# Seeing is believing

Steve came closer and got right up in my face. "What if we did something to convince you those old stories were real, Andy?"

"Yeah, what if we did that?" Mark and Ray said at the same time, going along with whatever Steve said, as usual. The three of them moved closer so that they surrounded me.

"Come on, guys," I murmured. "Cut it out. I didn't mean to make fun of your stories. Let's just forget about it, okay?"

Then something really bizarre happened. A dense cloud moved across the sky and everything got really dark. For a moment—just for a second— a ray of light penetrated the blackness, and Steve and his friends looked different. I know it sounds crazy, but for an instant they weren't kids my age. They looked like little old men. Really ugly, mean-looking little old men.

# CYBER ZONE

## Virtual Nightmare

# CYBER ZONE

## Virtual Nightmare

### S. F. Black

Art direction by Fabia Wargin.
Cover art by Peter Scanlan.

Printed in the United States of America.

10 9 8 7 6 5 4 3 2 1

# Chapter 1

"Hey, watch out!" I yelled.

I dodged to avoid getting wiped out by a little goblin on a bicycle. As he streaked by, I saw that the kid had tied a toy horse's head to the handlebars. He might as well have been riding a bucking bronco for all the control he had. "Put the training wheels back on," I muttered under my breath.

To make matters even worse, the kid had thrown the cape of his costume over his head. He screamed, "I'm the Headless Horseman! I'm the Headless Horseman!" as he rode around terrorizing everyone.

The first and second graders had taken over the Sleepy Hollow schoolyard. Mr. Blue, our very misguided assistant principal, had allowed the younger kids to wear their Halloween costumes to school. They were all so excited that they were practically bouncing off the walls. We were overrun by a bunch of pint-sized ghosts, goblins, and skeletons.

I pulled my coat collar up around my neck. The autumn air was cold, with the kind of dampness that cuts right into your bones. The sky was a chilly gray, yet it glowed with an eerie light, as if a storm were threatening.

The weather hadn't dampened the spirits of my friends Steve, Mark, and Ray. They stood there grinning in the middle of the after-school chaos. "Check out the little kids," Mark said. "Aren't they great?"

"Yeah," I said, though I didn't really mean it. I put my hands in the pockets of my coat as I watched the kids tearing around. The sight of their costumes annoyed me. They were all so boring. Nobody dressed up as anything cool, like a space alien or a robot, the way the kids in my old school did.

My twin sister, Amy, and I had moved to Sleepy Hollow with our parents earlier in the year. My dad had taken a job as a salesman for the Sleepy Hollow Mattress Company. "You'll sleep like Rip Van Winkle," is their slogan. Pretty silly, huh? Who would want to sleep as long as Rip Van Winkle?

Ever since we'd moved in, we'd been hearing how Sleepy Hollow was full of old legends and superstitions. As Halloween approached, it got worse. Kids were constantly talking about how someone's great-great-great-great grandmother knew Rip Van Winkle personally, or that someone's great-great-great-great grandfather had actually seen the Headless Horseman. It really bugged me. We'd even had to learn about the old legends in school. Lots of them were written down by a guy named Washington Irving. We'd been doing a whole unit on his stories—but I'd been goofing off in a major way.

I already knew the story of Rip Van Winkle from when I was a little kid. We were supposed to read "The Legend of Sleepy Hollow" for English class, but I kept putting it off. When my teacher, Mrs. Rathbone, discussed the story in class, I tuned her out.

Amy thought it was cool that people in town were preoccupied with old ghostly tales, but I didn't. I didn't believe in ghosts, and I thought ghost stories were dumb. That's what I'd been telling everybody, but lately, I had to admit, the stories had started giving me the creeps. I can't explain it, but sometimes I had the feeling that someone—or something—evil was watching me. Maybe I'd been in Sleepy Hollow too long.

Anyway, I was much more interested in the future. I loved science fiction and computers and wondering about whether people would be able to clone themselves. But I didn't get much chance to talk about those things in Sleepy Hollow—especially around Halloween.

Ray nudged me back to reality. "Try some of these," he said, pouring some Halloween candies into my palm. He held one up. It was a chocolate horse with a headless rider. "They're called 'Headless Delights,' after the Headless Horseman," he said.

I groaned. Ray ignored it.

"My dad says he saw the Headless Horseman once, when he was a kid. The guy rode up next to him, and the horse reared up and neighed. My dad managed to get away and hide, though. Isn't that the coolest? The Headless Horseman has been haunting Sleepy Hollow since the Revolutionary War. Dad says you definitely have a good chance of running into him if you're out alone on Halloween. Maybe I'll see him this year." Ray's face was all lit up.

"Oh, come on, Ray, get real," I said, unable to control my impatience. "You're not a little kid anymore. You should know there's no such thing as the Headless Horseman. It's just a story. Nothing is haunting Sleepy

Hollow because there are no such things as ghosts."

As soon as the words were out of my mouth, I hated the whiny tone of my voice, but I just couldn't make myself shut up. I kicked at a pebble. "Why is everybody here always talking about those dumb old stories from hundreds of years ago?"

The other guys exchanged glances that said *There he goes again* louder than any words could have. I'd seen those looks plenty of times before in the few months I'd lived here.

"It's fun to talk about spooky old legends around Halloween. What's the big deal, Andy?" Steve asked, with an edge in his voice. He tossed his head to flick his sandy brown hair out of his eyes. Steve was the shortest guy in the group. He was also the leader.

"Yeah, what's the big deal?" Mark and Ray echoed. I knew Steve was the leader because Mark and Ray always went along with whatever he said.

I couldn't hold back a sigh. *Why didn't I just keep my mouth shut when they started talking about those old stories?* I asked myself. Steve always copped an attitude when I said I didn't like them, as if he took it personally. Naturally, that meant the other guys gave me a hard time, too.

I sighed again. Hanging out with these guys had been a lot more fun before Halloween rolled around. Steve Talbot, Mark Harrison, and Ray Vandeveer were the first friends I'd made in Sleepy Hollow. Lately, though, I had the feeling they didn't like me very much.

I wished I could make the guys understand the way I felt. I didn't have time to try, though, because Steve started talking again. "Hey, have you guys checked out the new chat room yet?" he asked enthusiastically.

I didn't have to ask which one he meant. The only Internet chat room anybody logged on to anymore was *the* chat room. A local newspaper had set it up so people could talk about Halloween plans and tell scary stories—especially legends about Sleepy Hollow. It was called *Holloween*—like *Halloween*, but *Hollow* instead, for *Sleepy Hollow*.

While the other guys started talking about the chat room, I just shook my head. I wasn't particularly interested in getting on-line to talk about the same old stories that bored me to death all day. But knowing my friends would try it, I had decided to check it out the night before.

I'd only gotten as far as the home page, which was a picture of the Headless Horseman. Real original! Anyway, before I'd even gotten into the chat room, my computer had started acting really weird, making noises I'd never heard before. I'd managed to log off, but I was afraid my computer had gotten a virus from the chat room. My dad had promised to bring me an antivirus program that night.

Steve was looking at me with narrowed eyes. "Why haven't you tried *Holloween*, Andy? You think there's nothing to the stories, but the rest of us know they aren't just stories—some of the stuff is real. I guess you're too cool to think so."

*Here we go again,* I thought. "Aw, come on, Steve, don't put it like that," I said. "It's not because I think I'm too cool."

"Never mind. Don't try to explain," Steve said. I didn't like the way he was looking at me. My stomach started to

11

churn up what was left of the cafeteria meat loaf I'd had for lunch.

Steve came close and got right up in my face. "What if we did something to convince you those old stories were real?"

"Yeah, what if we did that?" Mark and Ray said at the same time, going along with whatever Steve said, as usual. The three guys moved closer so that they surrounded me. I shifted my feet. I didn't want to look scared, but I was.

"Come on, guys," I murmured. "Cut it out. I didn't mean to make fun of your stories. Let's just forget about it, okay?"

Then something really bizarre happened. A dense cloud moved across the sky and everything got really dark, the way it does sometimes on chilly autumn days. For a moment—just for a second—a ray of light penetrated the blackness, and Steve and his friends looked different. I know it sounds crazy, but for an instant they weren't kids my age. They looked like little old men. Really ugly, mean-looking little old men in funny, old-fashioned clothes.

# Chapter 2

I couldn't believe my eyes. I was staring at three really strange-looking little old guys with squarish faces and thin, wispy hair. They were wearing leather vests, bow ties, and wide-legged pants.

A warning bell sounded in my head, clanging louder and louder. *Andy, you've lost it,* I told myself. *You've gone over the edge.*

I stood there, feeling totally creeped out. The whole thing was so strange, I was too stunned to be scared. I just blinked, stared, and rubbed my eyes.

Suddenly the cloud moved away. When I blinked again, Steve, Ray, and Mark looked like normal kids again.

My heart was beating fast. *I'd better get Mom to take me for an eye exam,* I told myself.

But I didn't believe there was anything wrong with my cyes. I was beginning to think my *mind* was playing tricks on me. And I knew those stupid stories were the reason I was imagining things.

"You look like you've seen a ghost, Andy," Steve said. He was smirking.

"Not quite," I replied, trying to slow my breathing.

Mrs. Rathbone had told us that a spell had been put on Sleepy Hollow long ago. She got a really scary, mysterious look on her face when she talked about it. She said that because of the spell, evil trolls awakened every year at Halloween and haunted the town. The creatures possessed terrifying powers. They could make people see things and hear voices. They could even make people disappear . . . *forever*. When Halloween was over, the trolls went to sleep again—until the next year.

When Mrs. Rathbone said that in class, I thought she was a little weird, but I had to admit that some strange things had been happening to me lately. Like seeing my friends turn into little old men just now, for example. That wasn't normal, was it? And sometimes, when I was alone, I was sure I heard somebody calling my name. But every time I turned around, nobody was there. It was spooky.

Could it be that I was falling under the curse of Sleepy Hollow? Nah. I didn't believe in that stupid spell. *I've just been listening to Mrs. Rathbone's stories too much,* I told myself. I was going to have to do a better job of tuning her out.

Steve's eyes bored into mine. "I warned you that people in Sleepy Hollow see strange things around Halloween. There *is* a spell on the town—just like Mrs. Rathbone said."

I could feel my scalp tightening and the hair on the back of my neck standing up. There was no way Steve could know what I thought I had seen.

A knot twisted in my stomach. He couldn't have tricked me into seeing things, could he?

I tried to laugh it off, but my laughter sounded tinny.

Steve, Mark, and Ray were all staring at me now. I tried to move away from their penetrating eyes. *Maybe I'd better start hanging out with some other guys,* I thought. I filed the idea in the back of my mind.

"Look, Steve," I said, "let's get back to the chat room. I think it must have some kind of virus. I tried to get in last night, but I couldn't get past the home page."

Steve raised his eyebrows. He and the other two guys exchanged glances. "I didn't have any problem getting in last night. Maybe someone put a spell on your computer." He shrugged. "You never know what can happen here."

Mark and Ray laughed, like they thought Steve had said something really funny.

I just stood there frowning. "Look, enough already, okay? It's probably just a computer virus."

"All right, all right. We were only fooling around," Steve said. "You can take a joke, can't you?"

"Sure. If it's funny."

Steve was hardly listening to me. He was looking toward the school building. "Well, well, well. Will you look who's headed this way?"

I followed his gaze and saw a sight that immediately took my mind off everything that had happened. Katrina Tasselhoff was walking across the schoolyard.

"She's definitely awesome-looking," I couldn't resist saying. Katrina had long blonde hair and huge blue eyes. Most of the guys, including me, thought she was the prettiest girl in the whole school. I was sort of hoping I might finally get up the nerve to talk to her at the school Halloween party that night. If I did, I hoped I wouldn't screw up and say something dumb.

As Katrina approached, our little group held our collective breath. We shouldn't have bothered. Katrina was only headed our way because she had to pass us to get somewhere else. She walked by without so much as a nod and went over to talk to Brandon Voss.

Brandon was athletic, good-looking, and also, I thought, a real pain. He thought he was way cooler than anybody else in school. He also got a big charge out of goofing on people. The first day of school, Brandon had come up to me and introduced himself. Then he'd told me my shoelaces were untied. When I'd looked down at my shoes, he'd pulled my baseball cap down over my eyes. His friends laughed until their sides hurt. My cheeks still burned with embarrassment when I thought about it.

"Don't worry, Andy. He'll be sorry," Steve said out of the blue. It was as if he had read my mind, and it got me feeling creeped out about him.

That's when it happened. An awful feeling rolled over me—rolled *through* me—and knocked all other thoughts right out of my head. It was pure panic. Suddenly I could feel my heart hammering. I went all cold inside, as if my veins were full of ice water.

The guys were still looking at Katrina. Then Steve shouted something to Brandon. I heard Brandon say something back, and then everybody started laughing.

The sounds seemed to blur together because the blood rushing through my head was making such a loud noise.

*Amy. Amy.* My sister's name echoed in my mind.

Something terrible was going to happen. I could feel it. Without a word, I turned and ran as fast as I could.

There's some kind of mysterious bond between Amy

and me. I can't exactly describe it. Maybe it's because we're twins. We both have dark, curly hair and green eyes. When we were little, people kept mistaking us for each other.

We don't just look alike—sometimes we *think* alike. Before we could talk, we had a kind of secret language only the two of us could understand. It wasn't words, just a bunch of looks and noises that we used to communicate.

When we got older, we stopped making noises. We even forgot all about our secret language. But we still had a special connection. For instance, when one of us got hurt, the other one usually knew. When one of us was happy or sad, the other one usually felt it. Sometimes we even had the same dreams. And each of us definitely felt it when the other one was in danger.

Something horrible was about to happen to Amy, and I had to save her. *Run, run, run. Faster, faster, faster,* I told myself as I sped off. I raced toward the edge of the schoolyard as if an invisible force were pushing me along. I ran blindly, letting the force show me the way to go.

As I ran, the question burned in my mind: *Where is Amy, and why is she in danger?*

I reached the edge of the schoolyard. Beyond it a hill sloped steeply down into the woods.

I saw what was wrong. The kid in the goblin costume had totally lost control of his bike. It was careening crazily down the hill. Right in its path was Amy, her head bent as she inspected the ground, probably looking for specimens to add to her leaf collection.

The whole picture flashed into my mind in a split second. In that instant I knew that if the kid hit Amy, they'd both be knocked into one of the huge boulders at the foot of the hill.

Every fraction of a second, the bicycle was picking up speed. I tried to shout a warning, but no sound came out of my mouth. The kid must have been too frightened to scream. The entire catastrophe was happening in silence. Even the bicycle didn't make a sound as it raced over the ground.

I stood as still as a statue, squeezed my eyelids shut, and pictured the whole scene in my mind. There was Amy, and there was the kid on the bike speeding toward her.

I gathered up all my energy and pushed it toward Amy. *Move, Amy, move,* I commanded her. I didn't tell her in words, or even in thoughts, but with *feelings*. I imagined a huge ball of energy pushing her out of harm's way.

A moment later I opened my eyes and saw Amy leap sideways into the air, out of the bike's path. It was as if she were being propelled by a rocket. She landed on her hands and knees several feet away.

The bicycle skidded past her and did a three-sixty as it slid along the ground. It bounced a few more yards and then tumbled to a halt in front of the boulders.

The little kid pulled himself out from under the bike and stood up. He started running up the hill toward me, all the time wailing at the top of his lungs.

Suddenly I felt weak in the knees, as if all of the wind had been knocked out of me. I knew Amy felt that way, too. I watched as she got up slowly and began brushing dirt and leaves off herself. She looked up the hill at me, and our eyes locked in silent understanding.

The little goblin reached me and grabbed on to my leg. His costume was ripped and so were his pants, revealing scraped knees underneath. Miraculously, he was all right.

I dried his tears with the edge of his costume, and he started to settle down. He began doing that hiccup thing kids do after they've been crying a lot. By then Amy had climbed up the hill. She began patting his head to try to calm him down.

When we looked around, we saw that Steve, Mark and Ray had walked over to check out what happened. Steve spoke up first.

"Hey, that was weird, the way you took off like that all of a sudden, Andy." He looked from me to the little kid to Amy and then looked back at me with a sidelong glance. "How did you know something was wrong?"

Amy and I exchanged quick looks. "I didn't," I said lamely.

"It almost seems like you knew there was going to be an accident," Steve said. Suspicion lurked in his eyes. I looked away.

Steve kept looking at me. Mark and Ray were staring, too. I scuffed my toe in the dirt and shrugged.

Then the goblin kid began playing and grinning as if the accident had never happened. He started down the hill toward his bike. The rest of us headed for the school buses.

Amy and I sat next to each other. All the way home we were quiet. I knew what we were both thinking—that we could never explain to anyone else what had happened, so it was best not to say a word.

I leaned back against the seat of the bus and closed

my eyes. Sending the desperate message to Amy had really knocked me out. There was no way I'd be able to talk to Katrina at the party that night unless I took a nap when I got home.

I began to daydream about what might happen at the party. I sighed as I saw myself talking to Katrina. She was smiling at me as we danced. Our eyes locked, I leaned in closer, and—

"Andy, wake up." Amy's voice broke into my daydream. "It's our stop."

We got up and moved to the front of the bus. I silently vowed to continue my dream the second my head hit my pillow.

But when we stepped off the bus at our stop, Amy turned to me and said, "Andy, you know that chat room everyone is talking about—*Holloween*? I have the strangest feeling something about it wants to hurt you."

All thoughts of Katrina suddenly disappeared. If Amy thought I was in danger, I had to stay alert—and stay away from the chat room.

# Chapter 3

"Ready to go?" my dad called up the stairs.

"In a minute," I called back. I was putting the finishing touches on my costume for the party. I'd taken a shower after dinner to help calm me down, but Amy's warning echoed in my head.

I stood in front of the mirror examining my Rip Van Winkle outfit. There was a corncob pipe in the pocket of my overalls. I also wore one of my dad's old flannel shirts that had shrunk in the wash, and a long white beard that we'd found at the costume shop in town. I'd topped the whole thing off with a hat my sister wore one year when she dressed up as a witch, but I'd really beaten it up by stomping and sitting on it all week. Now it looked as if someone had slept in it for twenty years.

I sighed. I'd had a terrific astronaut costume in mind to wear to the party. I'd been thinking about how to put it together for weeks. Then Steve had talked me out of wearing it. He'd said that everyone would think I was a geek. He'd even convinced me to dress up as Rip Van Winkle, though now, for the life of me, I couldn't figure out how he'd done it.

"You really look like Rip Van Winkle." Amy was

standing at the door of my room, wearing a pink ballerina costume.

"Thanks, I guess," I said. "That's a nice costume. You look great."

Amy smiled. "Thanks."

"Come on, you guys!" My dad's voice drifted up the stairs again. Amy and I grabbed our coats. One thing about my dad—he hates to wait.

When we got downstairs, Dad was bouncing the keys in his hand. "Have a great time," Mom called as we hurried out the door.

"We will!" I called happily.

I was sure this would be the best Halloween ever—until I entered the school gym.

I spotted Steve, Ray, and Mark right away. They weren't wearing costumes. They had on the same clothes they'd worn to school that day. I was about to go over and talk to them, but something stopped me. It was the way the three of them were staring at me. It made me feel weird, just like I had in the afternoon.

Then I looked around the gym and saw that a lot of kids weren't wearing costumes. The hair on the back of my neck began to stand up. *It's early,* I told myself. *Other guys must have gotten dressed up.*

At least all of the girls were wearing costumes. Across the room I saw Katrina Tasselhoff. She was wearing an old-fashioned dress with a lacy apron that made her look pretty, but I hadn't the faintest idea who she was supposed to be.

"What kind of costume is Katrina wearing?" I asked Amy.

"She's Katrina from 'The Legend of Sleepy Hollow,'"

Amy whispered back. "Can't you tell? The story has been assigned for weeks. Haven't you been doing your homework?"

"Get off my case," I muttered.

Katrina looked at me and smiled. The smile changed to a giggle and the giggle got bigger until it turned into a laugh. Then she whispered something to her girlfriend and pointed my way.

*Katrina's paying attention to me,* I thought. *But is it a good thing or a bad thing?* Something told me I wouldn't like the answer.

I watched as Katrina pointed to another guy and laughed. Then she whispered something to her girlfriend again.

I looked in the direction she had pointed. There was a guy standing by the door dressed in overalls and a long white beard. He was holding a corncob pipe. Rip Van Winkle.

*Well, it's not unusual for two people to dress up as the same character,* I told myself. *Especially in this dinky little town.*

I looked around at the decorations. Even though they reminded me of the boring stories I'd been hearing for weeks, I had to admit they were pretty good. There were huge cobwebs all over the place, with spiders and bats stuck in them. Someone had made a papier-mâché figure of the Headless Horseman on horseback, holding a head with flashing red eyes. Naturally, the decorations included the usual witches, ghosts, mummies, and haunted houses, too.

After a minute, I headed for the punch bowl. Ahead of me in line was another guy dressed like Rip Van Winkle.

Somebody else was carrying away a cup of punch. Rip Van Winkle again.

My eyes searched the room. There were two Rip Van Winkles standing in the corner. I saw three more in the middle of the gym. There must have been at least fifteen Rip Van Winkles altogether.

That's when it hit me. The *only* guys wearing costumes in the whole room were *all* dressed as Rip Van Winkle.

I headed over to where Steve, Ray, and Mark were standing. As I got closer, they all looked at me and turned away, laughing hysterically.

"Okay, what gives? What's so funny?" I asked.

"You!" Steve whooped. He and the others started laughing all over again, slapping their knees.

All around the gym other groups of kids were laughing. Katrina was clutching her sides and tears were streaming down her pretty face.

"Gotcha! We told as many kids as we could to dress up like Rip Van Winkle," Steve spluttered. It wasn't easy for him to get the words out because fits of uncontrollable laughter kept interrupting him. "Almost all the new kids went along with it. How gullible can you be?"

I could feel my face turning red. Inside, my blood was heating up, and my temper was ready to erupt like a volcano.

"Some friends you guys turned out to be," I said through clenched teeth. "I can't believe you set me up so everyone would laugh at me." In the back of my mind I was thinking that my chance to impress Katrina was gone forever.

Steve and the others didn't act the least bit sorry. "If you could have seen the look on your face!" Steve giggled. Then he calmed down suddenly, as if he'd run out of steam. He got super-serious. "It was just a joke, buddy."

"Yeah, can't you take a joke?" Mark and Ray asked in chorus.

I was so mad, I couldn't speak. I just turned on my heel and left the gym.

"You shouldn't go out there alone tonight, Andy," Steve shouted after me. "Remember what Mrs. Rathbone said. Weird things happen to people in Sleepy Hollow on Halloween night. Sometimes they even disappear. Nobody ever sees them again!"

I didn't reply. I didn't even turn around. Being abducted by aliens couldn't be any worse than the humiliation I'd suffered tonight.

*Those guys have some nerve,* I told myself as I started walking home. Dark clouds blocked the moon's soft glow, and the sound of my feet crunching on dry leaves made the dark night seem spookier.

It wasn't long before I regretted having left the party. It was a long walk to my house, and there wasn't a soul on the lonely one-lane road.

I told myself it was too late to turn back. The guys would tease me and say I was a dork who was too scared to walk home in the dark on Halloween. I just wished I could keep my heart from pounding and stop the foreboding chill from snaking up my spine. I'd grabbed my coat on the way out, but it couldn't warm my icy blood.

"Hey, Andy." I heard a voice call my name in a soft,

hissing whisper. I stopped dead in my tracks. It was the same voice I'd heard before. I looked around, but no one was there, as usual. *It's just the wind,* I told myself as I started walking again.

"Hey, Andy." The voice slithered around me once more. Then I was nearly lifted off my feet as a bony hand grabbed the hood of my coat.

# Chapter 4

I kicked and screamed and tried to pull my hood free, but the hand held on tightly. I could feel the cold, bony fingers and hard knuckles brush against my neck.

I reached behind me, grabbed the awful claw, and tried to pry it loose. Something snapped, and my heart did a double backflip. The thing came off in my hand!

For a moment I thought I would throw up and collapse at the same time. I didn't want to look at what I was holding, but something made me do it.

As my eyes focused on the thing, I realized I'd made a terrible, foolish mistake. I still felt sick, but now it was from shame and embarrassment instead of fear. My face burned in the chill, crisp air, and my breath came in short, frosty gasps.

I wasn't holding a skeleton hand. I was holding a bunch of old, gnarled twigs from the end of a dried-up tree branch.

"You are a major idiot," I said aloud. The tree branch had somehow caught in my hood, and my mind had done the rest.

My eyes searched the night as my racing heart began to slow down. For a moment I was glad I was alone. No one had seen me make a fool of myself. If they had, my life in Sleepy Hollow would have been worthless.

I ran the rest of the way home. The wind blowing through the bare branches sounded like the voice that kept calling my name.

*No way. I'm not turning around,* I told myself silently. I ran faster.

Was I relieved when I finally reached my house! Unfortunately, the feeling didn't last long. All of the windows were dark. There was no one there.

"Oh, *right!*" I whispered, and snapped my fingers. I had forgotten my parents had gone to a party and wouldn't be back for hours. And Amy was having a good time at the school party, so I couldn't count on her for company any time soon, either.

I found the spare key under the mat and turned it in the lock. I swallowed hard as I pushed the door open. The refrigerator hummed noisily, and a board creaked under my feet as I walked into the hall.

*It's just old house noises,* I thought. I wondered for a moment why those noises you don't even hear when it's daylight get loud and scary when you're all alone at night. Then I clicked on the hall light, hung up my coat, and headed upstairs.

The door to my room was open a crack. A greenish glow spilled out into the black hall. I crept forward and slowly pushed open the door.

The eerie glow was coming from my computer monitor. My breath caught in my throat. I hadn't left the computer on. I *knew* it.

Then I saw that the home page for the *Holloween* chat room was on the monitor. The gruesome picture of the

Headless Horseman was bathed in green light.

As I watched, the home page disappeared, as if an invisible hand had clicked the mouse. A ribbon of letters snaked across the screen. The message was from *Sleepy*, and it was addressed to *AstroBoy*.

*Hey, Andy, are you there? I'm really sorry about your costume. The whole thing was just a joke.*

I stared at the screen. *AstroBoy* was my on-line name. *Sleepy* was Steve's. I was surprised he had left the party. I sat down in front of my keyboard and began typing a message.

*It wasn't a funny joke,* I typed back. *You guys were really flaming me.*

*We didn't mean to flame you, man. I'm really sorry.*

*Me, too.*

The last two messages were from *Rayven* and *Marko*— Ray's and Mark's on-line names. Before I could respond to them, another message appeared from Steve.

*I followed you partway home and kept calling your name. How come you didn't answer, AstroBoy?*

I sat up straight in my chair. I was sure no one had followed me. Whenever I had looked around, nobody had been there. I groaned as another thought occurred to me. What if Steve had seen me kicking and screaming when I got stuck on the tree branch? I didn't want to think about that.

Suddenly, my eyelids felt heavy. The words on the monitor blurred into a big jumble of letters as I tried to keep my eyes open.

Another message flashed across the screen. I could barely read the words through my half-shut eyes. *Glad you got home safe, AstroBoy. Like I told you, legends say that people disappear from Sleepy Hollow and are never seen again. Especially on Halloween night.*

I felt a prickle of irritation. I yawned as I began blindly moving my fingers over the keys. *That's enough joking for one day, Sleepy,* I typed. *I already told you I don't believe your old stories. None of those things really happened.*

Immediately new letters winked back at me from Steve. *What have you got against old stories?*

I was getting sleepier by the minute. It wasn't a normal sleepy feeling, though. It was as if I were being hypnotized. My hands and arms felt rubbery as I typed my answer.

*People who only think about the past aren't ready for the future and exciting stuff like virtual reality. With computers, people can create whole new worlds. And space aliens are scarier than any hundred-year-old ghosts.*

My eyelids were closing. I was going to have to sign off soon. Why was I so tired?

*Those who don't learn from the past are doomed to repeat its mistakes,* came the message from Sleepy.

The letters danced before my eyes. The word *Sleepy* seemed to fill the screen. *SleepySleepySleepySleepy SleepySleepySleepySleepySleepySleepySleepySleepy SleepySleepySleepySleepySleepySleepySleepySleepySleepy SleepySleepySleepy* . . .

The *Sleepy*s seemed to weave and rock, hypnotizing me like a pendulum. I couldn't take my eyes off the words. My eyelids drooped. I began rocking back and forth in my chair. No . . . I was sitting still. The *chair* was moving back and forth! I felt as if I were in a boat, pitching and rolling with the waves.

Suddenly the *Sleepy*s vanished, and the *Holloween*

home page with the picture of the Headless Horseman appeared again. My stomach lurched. This time, the horse reared up on its hind legs and made an awful groaning sound.

You'd think that would have jolted me out of my trance, but it didn't. I just stared at the screen, unable to move.

Then the whole room began to spin faster and faster, as if I were being swept into the eye of a tornado. The next minute I was flying through the air, spiraling down into the unknown.

# Chapter 5

I was inside a spinning tornado made of light. Shapes, forms, and colors flew by me at dizzying speeds. It felt like I was being sucked into a giant vacuum cleaner, pulled along faster and faster.

Then I heard that voice calling to me.

"Hey, Andy. Hey, Andy."

Somehow I turned my head. Steve, Ray, and Mark were flying along beside me.

"Isn't this great?" Steve cried. Mark and Ray were laughing, as usual.

"What's going on?" I somehow managed to get the words out.

Steve reached out and grabbed my arm. "We're flying through space and time. Actually, we're flying through *cyber*space. Isn't this the kind of thing you've always wanted to do?"

*How does he know?* The question popped into my mind. Then it popped right out again. Suddenly, it didn't matter.

I didn't care what was happening. I stopped being scared. I was having a fantastic time. It was like being on the best amusement park ride ever.

I watched Steve, Ray, and Mark laughing as they spun alongside me. I started laughing, too. I never wanted it to end.

But it did. Suddenly everything came to an abrupt stop, like the images on a TV or a computer screen do when you turn the machine off. All gone. Blank. There was no color, no picture, no light, and no sound. I was part of the blankness.

I didn't know how long it lasted, but finally I could open my eyes. I was lying on a hard, damp surface. I moved my hand over it. It felt like . . . the ground.

I blinked and started to get up.

*Uh-oh.* Something was wrong. *Dead wrong.*

I turned over and saw bare branches against a cold, gray sky. I jerked into a sitting position and rubbed my hands over my eyes. When I looked up again, the scene was the same.

I was sitting on a high hill surrounded by elm trees. The hill sloped gently toward a babbling brook. In the distance, I could see a tiny village. White smoke curled above red brick chimneys perched atop neat little houses.

I blinked and rubbed my eyes some more. *This is too weird,* I thought. I looked over my shoulder and saw that Steve, Mark, and Ray were just waking up, too, yawning and stretching.

I walked over and nudged Steve. "Will you look at that?" I said, pointing to the village. "Where do you think we are?"

"Sleepy Hollow," he answered without missing a beat. He wasn't the least bit rattled. He didn't even look surprised. Ray and Mark laughed.

A warning bell sounded in my head. These guys were far too calm. "Hey," I cried. "Is this another one of your jokes?" I looked around. *How did they pull this off?* "I don't like practical jokes," I mumbled.

More chuckles from the three guys. "Too bad, Andy," Steve said. "You're way too serious. You've got to lighten up and learn how to take a joke."

"Yeah," agreed Ray. "Because you're in one."

Now I was angry as well as confused. "This is crazy. I must be dreaming," I said. I gave myself the pinch test. I grabbed a piece of skin on my left forearm between my right thumb and index finger and gave it a healthy tweak. *"Owwww!"* I exclaimed as a big red welt rose on my arm.

The other three were still laughing. "It's not a dream," Steve said. "It's your worst nightmare. You've gone back to the time of Rip Van Winkle. Besides learning to like jokes, buddy, you'd better learn to like old stories, because you're in one of those, too."

Ray leaned toward me. "Think of it as an opportunity to be a part of history."

These guys were really beginning to get on my nerves. "This isn't funny," I said, trying to control my temper. "I don't know how you did this, but you can undo it. Take me home. Now."

For some reason this struck them as particularly hysterical. They fell on top of one another and started laughing all over again.

Then something awful—terrifying—happened. One by one the three kids stood up. They reached up to the tops of their heads and pulled down. It was as if each kid was unzipping a giant zipper. They unzipped right down the middle of their faces, down, down to the middle of their stomachs. They didn't stop until they reached their feet.

They peeled their skin back, and ugly, wizened creatures stepped out.

# Chapter 6

Standing before me were three little old men who looked like trolls.

A shock of recognition flashed through me. I realized that these were the same faces I had seen earlier that day on the playground.

All three creatures had wide, flat heads and greenish skin. They were wearing old-fashioned clothing—shirts with bow ties and pants with huge legs and buttons up the sides. The men didn't look cute, though. They looked mean—with mean, flat, piggy eyes and mouths twisted into sinister smiles.

The little old men giggled as they came toward me with their hands outstretched. "Now," said the one I knew as Steve, "we're going to play a game." His face looked positively evil, and he let out a cruel-sounding laugh.

"A game?" I echoed. My throat had suddenly gone dry, and my voice came out shaky. "You mean baseball or soccer? Frisbee, maybe? A video game?" *Fat chance,* I thought. I had a hunch I wasn't going to like any game these guys were into.

"Nope." Steve grinned. "We're going to play a very

*special* kind of game we made up ourselves a *long* time ago. We don't let just anybody play our game, Andy. You should feel honored."

He looked at Mark and Ray and gave them a big wink. The two of them winked back, like they were all sharing a joke. They weren't about to let me in on it, either. They started giggling again.

I was really sick of being goofed on, but I could see that I didn't have many options at this point. "How do we play?" I asked, more to cut out the *ho ho-ho-ing* than from real interest.

Steve began circling me, staring at me all the time with his little piggy eyes. "Listen up, because I'm only going to say this once. To win the game, you have to get back to the present before you're one hundred years old. You'll have to work fast. When time runs out—" he snapped his fingers—"you lose the game. Got it?"

I could feel my shoulders sag. "Could it really take that long to figure out how to get back? That's practically *forever.* I can't wait that long!"

Steve grinned again. "It's not *that* long. Besides, it's later than you think!" All three trolls chuckled.

I couldn't take any more of that high-pitched laughing. I stuck my hands in the pockets of my overalls and gritted my teeth. "What happens if I lose the game?" I asked, glaring at them.

"Well, *duh!*" Steve hit the side of his head with his hand. "It stands to reason that if *winning* means you get back to the present, then *losing* means you stay here. Then you'll find out how long forever is, Andy, and it's longer than a hundred years, I promise you."

For a moment I felt myself giving in to terror. I forced

the lump in my throat back down. "I don't believe your crazy story. This has got to be a dream—a nightmare. A person can't get stuck in the past."

Then I jumped to my feet. A choked laugh escaped my lips. "Wait a minute. You really had me going there. This isn't even the past—it's the story of Rip Van Winkle, right? It's not *reality*."

That really cracked them up. "I guess I'd better spell it out for you," Steve hissed. "You *are* trapped in the past, and it *isn't* reality. It's *virtual* reality! The unreal has been made real. Anything is possible here—even your worst nightmare."

My knees started to shake. I tried to take deep breaths to calm myself down, but I just couldn't get a grip on the fear that was washing over me.

"Don't look so glum, Andy," Steve said. "I thought virtual reality was your thing."

I tried to sound like I wasn't scared at all. "This is completely crazy. Nobody way back in time knew about virtual reality."

Steve shook his head again. "Wrong again. *We* are from way back, and we know all about it."

He came close to me. "Where do you think people go when they disappear and are never seen again?" He looked at me the way a teacher would look at a slow learner. "Come on, Andy, think. I told you before, when we were on our way here."

"Cyberspace?" I whispered incredulously.

The three guys began guffawing, patting each other on the back and giving each other high-fives.

"An *A* for the day!" Steve said. He opened his eyes wide and stepped closer to me. "I didn't think you had a chance in a million of winning our little game, but maybe there's hope yet.

"Let me explain something to you," he continued. "Way back, we used a lot of tricks to make people disappear from the present. We used hokey gimmicks like putting them in dream worlds or enchanted forests. For a while we got hooked on using the Bermuda Triangle, but that finally got old. The biggest bore of all was having people simply vanish into thin air." He faked an exaggerated yawn.

My head was reeling. I was incapable of moving even if I had wanted to.

"Anyway," Steve went on, "then came the information superhighway, and we"—he gestured to his two friends, then tapped his own chest—"were ready for it. Technology opened up new vistas. We could create virtual worlds in which to play our games."

"You mean I'm a character in a virtual reality game?" My voice fairly squeaked.

"Slap me five, my man," Steve said.

"I don't believe it." My voice shook. "If this is virtual reality, where are the goggles, the gloves? Don't we need sensor suits? Modules?"

More of those dumb giggles from the little guys. "We're *waaaayyy* past that," Steve replied. "Back in your present, they won't catch up to us for a long time. It's all yours to enjoy now, though."

For the first time I realized that Steve was carrying something. Now he held it up. "We brought you here through this. It's a special model."

I crept closer and stared at the object in his hands. It was a small computer. "It looks like an ordinary laptop,"

I said. "What's so special about it?"

The three trolls exchanged glances. "Well, you came through it to get here," Steve explained. "Isn't that special enough? You can't do that with an ordinary computer!" They all laughed.

Their laughter ripped through me. "Cut it out!" I snapped. When they quit laughing, I said, "I don't get it. How did I come through that thing?"

Steve wagged his finger in my face. "*Ah-ah-ah,* don't be so nosy. That's for me to know and for you to find out." He looked pleased with himself. Those awful little eyes were twinkling. "All you need to know is that if you win the game, we'll take you back through the computer to the present. Don't worry."

"Don't worry," I echoed. *Sure thing,* I thought. My arms hung limply at my sides. I was in total shock. I couldn't move a muscle.

Steve grabbed my right palm in his left hand and slapped it with his other hand. "You've got to get into the spirit of the thing," he said. "Now listen to this." He turned to the other two trolls. "Hit it, guys."

The three of them began to dance around as they chanted:

> *Before one hundred you must see*
> *The specter by the hanging tree,*
> *And meet the woman, cold and pale;*
> *Foil them both and do not fail.*
> *Then face one final enemy*
> *Before you mark a century.*
> *Defeat this foe and win the game,*
> *Or else it's here you will remain.*

"I hope you were listening carefully," Steve said when they were through. "I made it up myself. It's loaded with clues to help you win the game."

I stamped my foot in frustration. "It's in some kind of code. Who's the 'specter by the hanging tree,' or the 'woman, cold and pale'? And who's the 'final enemy'?"

"Oh, come on now." Steve threw his hands in the air. "We can't give everything away, or it wouldn't be any fun." He tapped his forehead with his index finger. "Think, think, think—that's the key. Here, this will help you, too." He handed me a dog-eared copy of "The Legend of Sleepy Hollow."

I threw the book on the ground. "This isn't fair!" I yelled.

"Not fair, not fair," Mark and Ray mimicked in a nasty singsong.

Steve tilted his head to one side. "Now, be a good sport, Andy. We've given you plenty of clues." He picked up the book and handed it to me again. Angrily, I stuck it in my pocket.

Then Steve twirled his hand in the air, and a mirror appeared. It not only appeared, it hovered in the air *all by itself*.

*"Ta-da!"* he said. "And now for your biggest clue! Take a look in the mirror!"

Cautiously, I approached the reflective surface and gazed into it. What I saw made my heart pound so hard that I feared it would burst through my chest. My whole body trembled so violently that my teeth practically chattered right out of my head.

I saw furrowed wrinkles in my forehead and deep creases extending from my nose to the sides of my mouth. My hair had gone ashen gray. I held my hands up in front of me. They were thin, with skin beginning to sag and fold.

A horrifying thought tore through my mind. *I am an old man!*

A shrill, jagged scream of terror tore from my throat. As it ripped through the air, I felt my knees collapse under me.

# Chapter 7

"Wow, we really scared him." Steve giggled. "Isn't that marvelous?" The three trolls began patting each other on the back and giving each other high-fives all over again.

The sight of Steve and his buddies laughing at me made me furious. How dare these twerps scare me out of my wits?

I was even madder than I was scared. I scrambled to my feet, seething with rage. I staggered toward the trolls, my arms outstretched, ready to grab one of them and wring his little neck.

Then my eyes rested on the laptop. Steve had left it lying next to a bush.

*Take it.* The thought flashed into my mind.

Adrenaline was pumping through my veins. I acted blindly, without thinking. My hand shot out and grabbed the laptop. I tucked it under my arm like a football as I turned and ran.

My clunky Rip Van Winkle shoes—Steve and his buddies had enhanced my costume for their game—clomped over the ground. I soon started huffing and puffing. After all, I wasn't twelve anymore. Judging from the way I looked in the mirror, I was at least sixty years old and in pretty bad shape.

The trolls were chasing me. I could hear the thumping of their fat little feet. They made squealing noises as they ran, like a herd of noisy rats.

Luckily, my long legs and head start gave me an advantage over them in spite of my age. I was able to keep well ahead of them until I reached a grove of trees. I crouched behind one of the tree trunks and waited, struggling to keep my out-of-breath wheezing quiet.

Finally the trolls raced past me. I waited a few moments longer and then sank to the ground. I leaned my back against a tree and took in great gulps of air.

I looked down at the laptop and smiled. I hadn't thought about what I would do with it when I stole it, but now I knew. The only person who could help me was my twin, Amy—though I hadn't the faintest idea how. I had to try to get in touch with her.

I opened the laptop and turned it on. It was easy to figure out how it worked. Although it was a lot smaller and more high-tech-looking than computers in the present, and it had some keys I didn't recognize, lots of things were basically the same as on other laptops I had seen.

I quickly e-mailed a message to Amy. *Help! I'm not sure where I am!*

As I clicked on *Send,* I tried to imagine how Amy and I communicated silently with feelings. I tried to use all of my energy to "think" the message through the computer. It had a long way to go.

There was no way of knowing if Amy would get the message, or if Steve and his buddies would intercept it.

I'd just have to wait and hope she would e-mail me back.

Suddenly I felt terribly tired. I knew it was because I had used up so much energy willing the e-mail to Amy. I stretched out on the ground and fell into a deep sleep.

When I felt myself stirring awake some time later, my first thought was, *What a terrible dream!*

My second thought was, *I am completely and totally starving.*

I rolled over and pulled the covers up around my shoulders . . . or tried to. There were no covers.

My eyelids sprang open.

*This is no dream. This is a virtual nightmare and I'm stuck here.*

I turned my head. Next to me the computer was on, and a message was blinking on the screen. *Mail is waiting.*

I sat up and punched the keys to bring it up. There was only one message. *Smart move, stealing the laptop, Andy. We were hoping you would try it, but we didn't think you'd have the nerve. Excellent work! Let the game begin!*

*You guys are sick,* I typed, and I clicked on *Send*.

*Thanks.* The letters appeared in a message box on the screen.

*Very funny,* I thought grimly.

Then more letters appeared. *You'd better start thinking about the rhyme, Andy. You're not getting any younger.*

I stared at the message in disgust. Then I clicked the mouse and it disappeared. I didn't want to talk to those guys anymore just then.

My stomach rumbled. *How many years has it been*

*since I've eaten?* Strangely enough, that thought struck me as so funny that I almost laughed.

I decided the first thing I'd have to do was find food. Then I could tackle the problem of how to get back to the present.

I tucked the laptop under my arm and started walking. My steps were slow and unsteady. I kept my eyes focused on the village in the distance and hoped that someone would take pity on me and give me something to eat.

I walked over several shallow brooks that looked very much the same. Then I came to a swamp. Since there was no way around it, I was forced to go through it.

Inside the swamp, the air was quiet and still. Crickets and toads chirped and warbled somewhere along the murky banks. Dead trees stretched their broken branches into the sky. The earth was damp and soft. My clumsy shoes sank into the clinging mud. Here and there cypress trees trailed webs of moss over the ground.

A snake slithered by me. A little later I saw an alligator that paused for a moment, looked me over, and then skittered away. By then I had figured out that this was no ordinary swamp. Too many things in there didn't belong in Sleepy Hollow in autumn, past or present.

I remembered what Steve had said about virtual reality. *The unreal made real.* The virtual world could be anything the trolls wanted it to be.

When I finally got out of the swamp, I searched the horizon for the village. My heart sank. It looked just as far away as before.

The wind blew softly around me. It sounded like the laughter of those creepy little guys.

I gritted my teeth and kept walking, over rolling hills and past fields of wheat. Then I passed by a field of golden corn.

Still the village looked as far away as before. The sun was in the same place in the sky. The wind blew again, and again it sounded like laughter.

*Okay, okay,* I thought. *I know what's going on. The trolls are programming the virtual reality scene here as I go along. They're manipulating space and time. How am I ever going to get out of here if they keep cheating like this?*

When I reached the edge of the cornfield, I saw a sprawling farmhouse sheltered by a giant elm tree. Beside it was a pond in which geese were swimming. Across from the farmhouse was a huge barn with a yard full of chickens and pigs. As a precaution, I slipped the laptop into one of the huge pockets of the coat Steve had thoughtfully provided me with.

A worker in overalls stuck his head out of the barn. "Howdy, old-timer!" he called.

I nodded back. *So I'm an old-timer at twelve,* I thought grimly. *If only you knew the truth, pal.*

Suddenly I *felt* like an old-timer. Although I'd figured I must be around sixty in virtual reality time, after all the walking I'd done I felt seventy-five.

The village still looked as far away as before. Maybe the little guys would never let me reach it—but I had to try. Besides, what else was there to do?

I kept walking. Lucky for me, I passed an apple tree. I scooped up a couple of apples and chomped on them as I trudged on.

It wasn't long before I came to a little wooden church

painted white. At least, it was once white. Now the remaining paint was brownish, and it was peeling everywhere. Beside the church was an overgrown graveyard. Broken headstones littered the bare ground, staring blankly at me.

All at once, a chill fell over me, as if a cold wind had blown through my body. The sky began to darken. Within seconds, night had fallen around me like a shroud.

My teeth began to chatter. A full moon rose in the sky, lighting up the ancient gravestones with eerie fingers of light.

I bent down to read the stones. *Balthus Van Meer, 1730–1782; Jan Brinker, 1760–1796; Hans Morgan, 1757–1798; Agnes Van Brundt, 1765–1785.*

My eyes were drawn to a small gray headstone behind the others. I peered through the darkness to read the name. I read the inscription twice, not quite understanding what it meant. Then a horrified scream escaped my lips. The gravestone read *Andy Winkler.* It was mine!

# Chapter 8

**S**uddenly the sky grew light again. I blinked. The headstone with my name on it had vanished. I struggled to slow down my racing pulse. *The little men must have had a good time with the graveyard trick,* I thought, disgusted.

After several minutes, my breathing slowed and I felt better. I walked on and crossed over a wooden bridge. I looked around and sensed that there was something familiar about all of this—the farm, the church with the gravestones in the yard, and the bridge. But how could that be? "What is Steve up to?" I muttered as I continued toward town.

I was glad when I came to a low log building and heard the sound of voices pouring from the windows. "Eight times eight is sixty-four, nine times nine is eighty-one."

*It must be a school!* I thought. I crept closer and peered in the window.

It was like no school I had ever seen in real life. This was an old-fashioned one-room schoolhouse. In the front of the room, behind a clumsy old wooden desk, stood the teacher. He carried a long, thin birch rod that he slapped against his palm again and again.

The teacher was a strange-looking guy. He was tall and skinny, with arms so long that his hands and wrists stuck out way below the ends of his sleeves. His head was too big for such a skinny body, and kind of flat on top. Huge ears stuck out from his head, and he had a long, bent nose and glassy green eyes.

"Mr. Crane! Mr. Crane! Could I please be excused?" one of the raggedy kids begged.

The teacher rapped the birch rod so sharply on the desk that I nearly jumped out of my clunky shoes. "No, you may not be excused!" he snapped. "You sit right there and pay attention, or I'll give you a good thrashing with this rod," he said in a screechy voice.

*That teacher should be arrested and thrown in jail,* I thought.

Just as I was about to turn away, something about the face of the kid who had asked to be excused made me stop short.

*I know him!* I realized suddenly. The shock of recognition went through me like a thunderclap.

What was that kid's name? He was a big jock from school. Katrina something-or-other was always talking to him.

I frowned. Why couldn't I remember Katrina's last name? Why couldn't I remember this kid's name at all? I was positive I knew him.

*Well,* I reasoned, *with all the things that have been happening, it's a wonder I remember my own name.* I repeated it to myself a few times. *Andy Winkler. Andy Winkler. Andy Winkler.*

The teacher didn't do any thrashing, in spite of his

threats. All of a sudden he didn't look angry anymore. He pointed to the door and told the kid to get out, which he immediately did. He ran right past me.

"Hey, you!" I called. "Wait! What's your name?"

The boy stopped and gave me a squinty-eyed look. "Brandon Voss, as if it's any of your business," he said.

I was too happy to let the snotty comment bother me. I started clapping and jumping up and down. "Yes, yes! That's it! *Brandon Voss*—I remember now!"

Brandon's features clouded with suspicion. "Don't be afraid!" I said quickly. I didn't want him to run away before I had the chance to explain. "Brandon, it's me, Andy Winkler! It's Andy from Mrs. Rathbone's English class."

Brandon backed away. "Who's Mrs. Rathbone?" He tilted his head to one side.

"Our English teacher!" I ran up to him. "Don't be afraid, Brandon. Don't pay any attention to the way I look. The little guys changed me when they brought me here. How come they didn't change you?" I babbled, my words tumbling over each other.

I waited for a look of recognition to dawn on Brandon's face. It didn't. Instead, he sneered at me.

"You're nuts, old man. You've lost your mind," he said. "I don't know anything about a Mrs. Rathbone. My father is a barrelmaker, and I've lived right here all my life." He turned and began walking off.

"Brandon, wait!" I grabbed his arm. With that, the kid really went ballistic.

"Leave me alone, you crazy old coot!" he shouted. He kicked me in the shins before he ran away.

I stared after him, my mouth hanging open.

Then a terrifying thought struck me. I had a feeling I knew why Brandon didn't remember my name, and why I hadn't remembered his.

It was a part of the game that the little guys had decided to let me figure out on my own. The longer I was here, the more of my memory I lost. That must have happened to Brandon. Steve had probably programmed Brandon's virtual world differently from mine. Maybe Brandon had been in his virtual world longer, and he'd forgotten everything in the present.

Terror gripped my throat as I realized how the game was stacked against me. Soon I wouldn't remember anything about the present. Once that happened, I'd stop trying to get back there.

# Chapter 9

"**O**ut of the way! Coming through, old-timer!"

I moved aside as a big guy pushing a wagon full of barrels rattled by me. I scratched my head. Maybe that was Brandon's "dad."

I had finally reached the village after what seemed like hours of walking. Up close, it was still small. The houses were made of yellow bricks and had shuttered windows and shingled roofs. The rows of houses were all so neat and clean that they didn't even look real.

*They aren't real!* I reminded myself.

As I strolled, I checked out the kids my own age. They were working hard, lifting and carrying and shoveling. None of them looked happy.

*What do they do for fun here?* I wondered. *It must be a real drag with no television and no radio, no movies and no pizza, no place to go like the . . . like the . . .*

My mind searched frantically for the right word. "Place to shop, place to shop," I murmured, trying to focus my mind. "You go there with your friends, you hang out, you cruise."

Two women wearing bonnets on their heads and aprons over their long dresses passed by me and giggled.

"Crazy old fellow is talking to himself," one whispered loud enough for me to hear.

Suddenly, the word came to me. *"Mall!"* I blurted. *"Mall! Mall! Mall!"*

The people around me scattered in all directions. "Don't go near him," a young woman said to her son. "He's daft."

I didn't care what she called me. I was too busy telling myself that I wouldn't forget things. Not like Brandon Voss had.

"I won't forget, I won't forget," I repeated through clenched teeth.

It was really a bummer that Brandon Voss didn't remember my name or where he came from. Between the two of us, we might have been able to figure out how to win this so-called game.

Maybe Brandon wasn't my favorite person in reality, but here in virtual reality, he had seemed like a long-lost friend. Now I had no one.

My head swiveled right and left as I walked down the dusty main street. I secretly hoped that somebody else from the present was stuck here.

My heart skipped a beat. At the corner I saw a tall, skinny woman carrying a basket of apples. Her dark hair was tightly pulled back from her head and hidden under a gingham bonnet. Her eyes looked startled, the way my teacher's eyes always did.

I stared hard at the woman. Could it really be Mrs. Rathbone? She sure walked like Mrs. Rathbone, with those little shuffling steps. But I couldn't be sure. After all, I didn't have the eyesight of a twelve-year-old anymore.

The lady stopped to talk to another woman. I hurried over, inching closer and closer.

The woman I hoped was my teacher turned her back. I touched her shoulder—just a tap to get her to turn around.

"Mrs. Rathbone? Mrs. Rathbone?"

*"Aaaagggghhhhh!"* the woman shrieked as she turned and looked at me. "How dare you come near me? Who are you?"

*"Shoo,* you old beggar!" the other woman cried, rushing at me and flapping her apron.

"Sorry. Sorry," I mumbled as I moved away from them.

The woman I thought might be Mrs. Rathbone glared at me as I walked away. Now I could see that she didn't look much like Mrs. Rathbone at all. I had only wanted it to be her.

I was truly all alone.

I soon passed a house that wasn't like the others. It was rundown, and the front door hung crookedly off the hinges. It looked as if no one had lived there for a long time.

Cautiously, I entered. The inside was even worse than the outside. There were several chairs made from some boards that were haphazardly hammered together. Sunlight peeked through gaping holes in the roof, and the mantle over the fireplace was chipped in several places. There were no pictures hanging on the peeling plaster walls, but the floors were swept and tidy.

On a table made of rough wooden planks stood a pot full of vegetables—potatoes and turnips, mostly. Probably they were for some soup or stew.

My hands shook and my mouth watered as I grabbed a potato, then a turnip, and took huge bites as fast as I could. I ate and ate, all the while stuffing more vegetables into my overalls.

Soon my pockets were full. I saw a burlap sack in the corner of the room. I grabbed it and began stuffing turnips and potatoes inside. There was a loaf of coarse bread next to the pot, and I took that, too. I knew I was stealing, but I was so hungry I couldn't help myself.

Suddenly I stopped and stood perfectly still. Every nerve in my body went on red alert.

Even before I saw the shadow on the floor, I knew that someone had entered the room. I felt sweat bead up on my forehead and trickle down my face. My heart pounded in my chest. I was afraid to turn around.

"Are you my father?"

I whirled around and saw a boy of about twelve in raggedy clothes. He had a round, freckled face, and he looked at me with wide, curious eyes.

"Your father? How could I be your father?" I asked.

The boy took a step toward me. "I guess you're not then," he said. "You're much too old to be my father, anyway. Maybe you're my grandfather?"

"Are you crazy?" I asked. "I'm probably the same age as you."

"Wha—?" The boy's jaw dropped. For a moment he looked totally shocked. Then he started laughing. "Ha! That's a good joke, Grandpa," he said.

"I am *not* your grandfather!" I screamed as I stamped my foot. Then I realized that I *did* look old enough to be his grandfather.

Another shadow darkened the door. A woman in a

long black dress and a black bonnet stood there scowling at me.

"What are you doing here, old-timer?" she snapped. She grabbed a ratty broom and came toward me, brandishing it in my face. Then her own face went pale and ashen. She stopped dead in her tracks.

"Why—is that you, Rip Van Winkle?" She came closer and looked into my eyes. "It *is* you," she whispered as her hand flew to her heart. "You've aged at least twenty years."

Suddenly her features changed. Her face reddened. "Why, you good-for-nothing, lazy man! How could you run off and leave us with no money and all this work to do?" She raised the broom over her head and started whacking me on the shoulders.

"Hey, cut that out!" I cried, putting my arms up to shield myself from the blows. "That hurts!"

Somehow I managed to get past the woman and her broom. I held the sack of food tightly and ran. "I'm not Rip Van Winkle! I'm Andy Winkler!" I called over my shoulder as I raced away.

"Go ahead and add lying to laziness!" she screamed as she ran after me. "Call yourself whatever you like. I know you're my worthless husband!" I felt a rock bounce off my back, then another, and another.

With every step I imagined what the woman would do to me if she ever caught up with me. It was nothing good.

The landscape flew by me—houses, trees, horses, farmland. Soon I came to the bridge near the church. My knees shook. Still, I forced myself to keep going. I had to put as much distance between myself and that horrible, crazy woman as possible.

It seemed that I reached the farmhouse with the huge barn and the geese in the pond in no time. *That's weird,* I thought. It had taken much longer to reach the village earlier. *The trolls are at it again,* I decided.

There was no way I could have run all the way from the village to the farmhouse when I was twelve. Now I was rattling along in the body of a sixty-year-old, and I was still running. I didn't know how it was possible, but I was glad.

Unfortunately, the sun was sinking rapidly, and soon I was running in the dark.

Then a wave of exhaustion hit me as hard as a whack with a sack of bricks. I stopped and leaned against the trunk of a huge, gnarled tree, coughing and wheezing, trying to catch my breath. I felt so tired, so old.

A tortured sound seemed to be coming from the branches of the tree. A horrible, human-sounding groan surrounded me. I jumped away from the trunk, horrified, afraid of what I might see.

I held my breath. The groan came again. My heart began to hammer in my chest. "This isn't real, this isn't real," I kept repeating to myself.

A flash of lightning snaked through the darkness. As the light exploded across the sky, I saw what had been making the horrible noise.

# Chapter 10

I screamed at the gruesome sight before me. Just as I was about to run, I heard a voice. "Take it easy, old fellow. Your eyes are fooling you. That's not a body hanging in the tree. It's just a gash in the wood where lightning struck a long time ago."

I looked around wildly. Where had the voice come from?

"That groaning must have spooked you," the voice continued. "It sounds scary, but it's only a couple of branches rubbing together. I ought to know. I've been hanging around here for a long time."

My eyes darted from side to side. Where was the owner of the voice?

Then I saw him. He was leaning against the tree as if he didn't have a care in the world. He was about twenty-five years old. He was dressed in a soldier's uniform like the ones you see in old paintings of the Revolutionary War.

"I d-didn't see you before," I stammered.

The soldier shrugged. "Oh, I've been here a while. Quite a while."

I figured that this place must be okay if a soldier hung

out here. I took a deep breath to steady myself. "Sure is spooky out here. Say—how did you know I thought I saw a body in the tree?"

"I guessed," he replied. "It's what most people who pass by think they see. Like I told you, I've been hanging around here a long time."

I stepped closer to him. He had a broad forehead and a jutting jaw. His eyes were deep and piercing. He would have been a pretty good-looking guy, I thought, except for his posture. His head tilted so far to the left that it nearly touched his shoulder.

"How come you like this place?" I asked.

A corner of the soldier's mouth lifted in a half smile. "I never said I liked it. This is just my place. By the way, my name is John. Where are you headed, old-timer?"

"I'm Andy." I held out my hand for a shake, but John didn't move to take it. I tried to pretend I was just going to scratch my head. "I'm not really an old-timer, though. I'm only twelve."

John cracked up. I guess I couldn't blame him. Even I was having a hard time remembering I was only twelve.

"How long have you been twelve? About seventy years?"

It seemed like everyone around here was prone to laughing fits. "Never mind," I muttered. "I was only kidding."

"That's a good one," he said. Then he calmed down. "You're all right, old fellow."

"What kind of uniform is that, anyway?"

John had been smiling at me, but now his eyes narrowed suspiciously. "Revolutionary War Army," he said. His brows knitted. "Is this another joke?"

"No!" I said hurriedly. "I'm just not up on my history."

Another weird look. "History? It wasn't *that* long ago. You must have been around for the war, old-timer."

It looked like I was putting my foot in my mouth every time I opened it. "Oh, right!" I said as I hit the side of my head. "I'm just a little forgetful sometimes. Say, we really kicked butt, didn't we? What did you think of George Washington?"

John frowned. "I didn't see much of him. My commanding officer was General Clinton."

*General Clinton.* I searched my mind for information about the American Revolution. I didn't remember any General Clinton. Too bad I hadn't paid more attention in Mr. Martin's history class.

I tried to fake it. "Well, he was something, wasn't he? Quite a guy, that General Clinton! Did you see a lot of action?"

"Hmm? What do you mean, *action*?"

"Action—battles, fighting."

John smiled knowingly. "Oh, you bet. Until they caught me, that is."

I could feel my eyes grow wide. "You got captured? Wow. What happened?"

John calmly raised a hand to his neck. "I was hanged. Right from this tree. I've been hanging around here ever since." John laughed, an evil, mocking laugh.

"You're *dead*?" I wailed.

No wonder John held his head at a weird angle. I started backing away.

John came toward me. Now that he didn't have the tree behind him, I could see that he was totally transparent. *A ghost.*

"I'm s-sorry the B-British hanged you," I stammered. "B-But that makes you a hero."

John kept coming toward me, staring at me with those piercing eyes of his. It was as if he were hypnotizing me. I couldn't move.

"It wasn't the British who hanged me," he hissed. "It was the Americans. I told you I fought with General Clinton. Everybody knows he was British."

John reached out and grabbed my throat in a powerful grip. He lifted me off the ground. "You really ought to keep up with the news more," he said. He began to squeeze my throat tighter and tighter.

# Chapter 11

I struggled, my legs flailing helplessly in the air. I tried to pry the dead soldier's hand loose, but his grip was too strong.

"I was quite angry when they hanged me," he said. "I promised myself I'd get back at the Americans. The trouble is, I have to stick around this tree, so I can only get my revenge on the occasional stranger who passes by."

John stared into my eyes. He drew his ghostly lips back from his teeth as he tightened his grip further. He was choking me!

I was growing weaker and weaker. I couldn't breathe at all anymore. I could feel myself starting to pass out. Then an incredible thing happened.

Somehow I mustered all my strength for one last, desperate struggle. I raised my hands to my throat and tried to pry the soldier's fingers away.

Power shot through me like a jolt of electricity. I felt incredibly strong.

When I ripped one of his hands from my throat, John looked at me, astounded. I kept pulling and soon broke the grip of his other hand. With a giant heave, I pushed the ghost away. Then I turned and ran as fast as I could.

The thud of my footsteps was the only sound I heard. Still, I didn't dare turn around. After all, John was a ghost. His footsteps wouldn't make any noise. For all I knew, he was flying in the air above me, just waiting to grab me again.

After a few seconds, though, I couldn't resist one brief backward glance over my shoulder. What I saw made me stop in my tracks.

John was still standing not far from the tree. He was jumping up and down and pounding the air in front of him with his fists.

I stood there watching. John was trying to come after me, but he couldn't do it. He was pushing against something invisible.

My mind was racing. I watched as John threw himself toward the invisible barrier. He bounced off and landed on the ground.

In a flash, I understood. John couldn't go far from where he was hanged. He was cursed to spend an eternity beside that tree. That's why he was always "hanging" around!

*The joke's on you, soldier boy,* I thought. I went closer and thumbed my nose at him. "Hey, what's the matter, John? Can't you catch me? Come on, I'm right here!" I did a little dance. I knew it was childish to gloat, but I couldn't help myself.

It wasn't long before I got tired of taunting John. In fact, I was just plain tired.

I started looking for a nice, soft piece of ground that wasn't haunted so I could get some sleep. There was a full moon in the sky, brighter than any I had ever seen.

Hundreds of fireflies danced in the air. The land was lit up almost like day.

I passed a small pond and suddenly realized that my mouth and my throat were as dry as dust. I got down on my knees and bent toward the water.

Suddenly I gasped and drew back. In the brilliant moonlight my face was reflected in the smooth surface of the pond as if I were looking into a mirror.

I had begun the day as an old man, but now I was even older than before. I had aged years in only hours. There was much less hair on my head. My eyes had sunk deeper into their sockets, surrounded by folds of skin and bags underneath.

I wasn't sure how old I was, but I was certain of one thing. Time was running out. Soon I would be trapped here forever.

# Chapter 12

I yawned. I stretched. How long had I been asleep?

For a few incredible moments, I thought everything that had happened to me was only a nightmare. I opened my eyes, expecting to see the ceiling of my room.

Instead I saw crows circling in the sky overhead. It all came rushing back to me—the chat room, the little men, the ghostly soldier who'd tried to strangle me. I sat up wearily.

I decided to check the laptop. When I pulled it out of my pocket and opened it, I saw a ribbon of letters appear on the screen.

*Congratulations, Andy! The magic number is eight-five. You're eighty-five years old today. Happy birthday. Time is running out, but you're playing a good game! You've really got a good head on your shoulders—get it?*

These guys were crazy. I was going to give them a piece of my mind—tell them exactly what I thought of them. I reached for the keyboard. Then my hands drew back.

I didn't have time for childish tantrums. I needed to find out how to get out of here.

I started typing. *How about another clue?* I wrote. I didn't bother signing my name. Steve and the others would know who the message was from.

In seconds the reply appeared. *No way. We've given you all the clues you're going to get.*

The screen went blank. The little guys had cut off communications. A whirl of frustration spun around inside me.

Angrily, I punched my knee with my fist. *"Ow!"* The cry escaped my lips. I had to be more careful not to hurt my eighty-five-year-old hands.

A whirring, humming noise filled my ears. It came from the computer! I hoped that Steve had had a change of heart.

A new message was on the screen. As I saw the name of the sender, *AmyJo,* I held my breath. That was Amy's on-line name. *Jo* was the name of her favorite character in *Little Women.*

My heart jumped into my throat. It was too good to be true! I had gotten through to Amy, and she was able to get through to me! I quickly read her message.

*I knew you were in danger. Where are you? How can I help? What's happening? Tell me everything.*

I could almost feel Amy's energy pulsing through the letters on the screen. I started typing quickly. *I'm here, Amy. I got your message.* I clicked the mouse on *Send,* using all my energy to push the message through the computer toward Amy. I waited.

I pumped my fist in the air as I saw letters ripple across the screen again. *I have to work hard to push the message through. Are you okay?*

*I'm fine—sort of,* I typed. My fingers flew across the

keys. *You were right about the chat room,* I typed. Then I told Amy about the strange little troll-like guys and how they had used the chat room to somehow kidnap me into cyberspace. I told her everything I could about the game and the village where the woman chased me and called me "Rip Van Winkle."

After several minutes of typing quickly, my old hands started to cramp. I sent the message, then gently massaged my fingers. Almost instantly, Amy's reply appeared on the screen. She had figured out something right away. I'd always known my sister was smart!

*It sounds like you're Rip Van Winkle, and you're trapped in "The Legend of Sleepy Hollow."*

I leaned over the keyboard. *So what about the woman who chased me?*

*Let me finish,* Amy typed. *You're trapped in a twisted version of "The Legend of Sleepy Hollow." Maybe you're Rip Van Winkle because you were wearing that costume when you were zapped into the computer. These little guys change things around whenever they feel like it, so that's why Mrs. Van Winkle is there.* The letters flashed at me. Then more appeared. *Did you ever read "The Legend of Sleepy Hollow"?*

I could feel myself turning red. I had a feeling Amy already knew the answer before I sent it. *No. The little old guys gave me a copy, though.*

When Amy's reply appeared, the letters themselves looked angry. *READ IT! It's obviously a clue.*

She was probably right. I had assumed the little guys had only given it to me as a goof, but maybe I should have figured it was a clue. Or was it? I started typing again.

*You know the story. Does it say anything about a soldier named John who was captured and hung by the colonists during the Revolutionary War and still haunts the place?*

*It sounds like Major André. I've heard people say he still haunts Sleepy Hollow.*

My fingers punched the keys. *Well, I think he tried to strangle me last night.*

I waited. When I read Amy's reply, my heart started to pound. *So that's why I had that awful dream. It felt like I was suffocating. Someone was strangling me, but I couldn't see who it was—I just felt hands around my throat. I thought I was going to die, but suddenly I felt very strong, and I was able to get free. My neck still hurts, and the muscles in my legs ache as if I'd been running a long time.*

My mouth dropped open as I read the words on the screen. It was that mysterious bond that Amy and I had— that strange communication. That's how I had gotten the strength to break John's grip on my throat. That's how I had been able to run from Mrs. Van Winkle. Amy had sent me strength through her dream.

My fingers moved over the keys. *You're here with me, Amy. You're helping me.*

Suddenly my eyelids felt like lead weights. I blinked as I read Amy's next message. *Sending e-mail this way is exhausting.*

I yawned as I leaned over the keyboard. Fatigue washed over me in a wave. I struggled against it, but it was no use.

Amy must have been feeling tired, too, for at that instant the computer screen went black. I fell over onto my side, and my eyelids snapped shut. In less than a minute I was fast asleep.

When I awoke, the sky was dark and cloudy. The temperature had dropped while I was asleep, and it was getting colder by the minute. I started shaking all over from the cold, and my teeth chattered.

As if things weren't bad enough, snow started to fall. There were little wispy flakes at first, but soon they got bigger and bigger and fell faster and faster. Pretty soon the snow was coming so thick and fast that I could hardly see my hand when I held it up to my face. The wind began to blow harder as I picked myself up and trudged through the woods.

The snow blew sideways through the trees and stung my face. Then I heard a sound that made me shiver even more than the cold. It was a bloodcurdling, awful shrieking, as if someone was being tortured.

The snow was piling up now. It was nearly as high as the tops of my big, old, clunky shoes.

Up ahead, a gigantic gray shape appeared out of the darkness. I could feel the hair on the back of my neck rise as I stared at the imposing figure.

Then I realized it was a combination of the snowstorm and my fear that had caused my eyes to play tricks on me. The shape was only a huge rock.

The eerie, high-pitched shrieking cut through the air again. I tried to run, but all I could do was slog slowly through the snow.

I shielded my eyes from the stinging flakes and pushed forward. I wanted to put as much space between me and the horrible sound behind me as I could.

But when I was on the other side of the rock, I heard the terrible wailing again. This time, though, it was in front of me instead of behind me.

"*Aaaahhhhhh!* I'm coooold, so coooold. I'm freezing to death! Come here and give me your warmth! Keep me warm!" cried the voice.

I turned to the right and trudged on. The heart-wrenching cry cut through the frosty air again. "Help me, please! I'm so cold! I'm freezing! Give me your warmth! I must have it or I will die!"

The sound was still coming from somewhere in front of me. I turned back the way I had come. Then the mournful wailing rang out yet again. Once more, it was coming from somewhere in front of me.

I spun around wildly. I realized it didn't matter which way I went. I couldn't escape the inhuman noise. It made me feel cold inside—colder than I had ever felt before.

The shrieking grew louder. It seemed to be in front of me, behind me, above me and below me, it even seemed to pass right through me. For a moment I thought I might go mad.

Then I saw what was making the awful sound. A figure was coming toward me, moving through the snow effortlessly, gliding along. It was a woman dressed in white. As she got closer to me, I realized that the rest of the woman was white and glittering, too. She was made of ice.

Long, thick icicles hung from her head. Frost coated the surface of her face, and more icicles dangled from her fingers.

I was powerless to move as she glided over the surface of the snow toward me.

"I'm cold!" the woman shrieked. Her breath came out in huge frozen clouds. I longed to back away, but I was paralyzed with fear.

"Don't be afraid," said the ghostly ice woman. "I'll make sure you don't feel a thing when I turn you into ice."

The woman reached out a thin, pale hand. Frost hung from the lashes of her ice-blue eyes.

Even before she touched me, my insides began to tighten up, slow down, freeze. When her finger touched my lips, I could feel my blood turning cold. My limbs were hardening.

The woman took my hand in hers. I saw my own hand becoming solid, shiny, transparent—ice.

# Chapter 13

The woman stared at me with her pale, frosty eyes, freezing my brain with her gaze just as her touch was slowly freezing the rest of my body. I struggled to pull away, writhing in her grasp.

The blood that flowed through my veins was turning to a liquid so cold that it actually burned. As my blood became ice, my movements grew steadily slower and stiffer.

I began to feel sluggish. My limbs turned rubbery, and then the rubber became hard and brittle. My arms and legs were icicles. As I froze, I saw the woman who held my hand begin to bloom with life as she drained the warmth from my body.

*Help me, Amy,* I thought. I was barely able to form the words in my mind. I hoped that somehow Amy would know I was in danger.

Suddenly a tiny spark flared to life in my brain. I thought about warm things—a roaring fire, a hot shower, cups of steaming hot chocolate—anything that would make me warm. The small flame inside me grew and grew, getting redder and hotter.

In an instant it had become a giant bonfire that

spread through my entire body, shooting out through my fingers and toes.

I was sure I could feel Amy's presence helping me. Together, we were making my body warm. My blood began to thaw, and I felt as if I were coming to life again. Soon I was able to move, and I looked at the hand that was held by the icy ghost. It was glowing red. In fact, my whole body was glowing as if I were made of fire.

The icy figure began to heat up, too—and fast. *Too fast*. Instead of coming to life, she was melting.

Parts of her face and body began to drip to the ground. A horrible wail escaped her lips.

I tried to let go of her hand, but I couldn't. It was awful. Within seconds, the ice woman was only a puddle at my feet. I was left clutching air.

Once the woman was gone, it felt as if the flame inside me had burned itself out. I was completely drained, and my old limbs just couldn't support my weight anymore. With a loud groan, I collapsed in a snowdrift.

# Chapter 14

I woke up screaming. "*Aaagggh!* I'm cold! I'm cold! I'm freezing to death! Help!"

Wait a minute—I wasn't cold, I realized after a moment. At least, I wasn't any colder than I usually was after spending the night outside on the ground in autumn. All of the snow had disappeared.

Compared with how I'd felt as a human ice cube, I was pretty comfortable—until I tried to sit up, that is. My arms rebelled when I tried to move them. Every part of my body was stiff, right down to my aching bones.

I remembered how Amy had told me her neck hurt and her legs ached after she helped me get away from Mrs. Van Winkle and Major André. She probably wasn't feeling too good this morning, I thought guiltily. I made a silent vow to do her chores for a week if I ever made it back to the present.

Then I spied the mirror hanging in the air. Steve and his cronies must have come around while I was napping. *Why is the mirror there?* I wondered uneasily. *Am I still eighty-five?*

My bony knees knocked together as I stood up. I hobbled over to take a look.

That was a mistake. Sure enough, I was years older than before. The surface of my face was so lined that my skin looked like a window screen. I barely had any hair left on my head—just a few wispy gray strands sticking straight up on top. And why hadn't I felt it when I'd lost a couple more teeth—and where had they gone? Somehow I didn't think the tooth fairy made her rounds in virtual reality.

Disgusted, I limped back to the laptop. I figured that the merry pranksters had left a message for me, and I was right.

*The magic number is ninety. Happy ninetieth birthday! Good morning, Andy.*

I was ninety years old. Time was *really* running out.

As panic washed over me, I began to feel faint. I sank to the ground, clutching my chest.

I took a deep breath—or, rather, I tried to. The effort of filling my lungs with air made me cough and wheeze. I tried again.

After a moment my breathing became slower and easier, and I stopped wheezing. Suddenly, I could feel Amy's presence, almost as if she were sitting next to me. I felt the panic lifting. Amy was here with me, lending me strength.

The laptop beeped. Another message appeared on the screen. I leaned closer to read it. *Score points for you. You managed to melt the ice woman, one of our favorite ghosts. This game is fun!*

I could feel my thin lips twisting into a sneer as a wave of rage swept through me. I didn't think the game was fun at all.

I got so angry that I grabbed the laptop and lifted it above my head, ready to smash it on the ground. Then I realized that if I did that, I'd have no way to communicate with my sister.

My sister . . . What was her name? I floundered for a moment. Then the answer came. Amy. *Amy.*

My skinny arms trembled as I lowered the laptop. I heard laughter—the little guys giggling. I leaned over the keyboard and typed, *You didn't tell me I'd start losing my memory.*

The reply flashed on the screen. *Can't you take a joke? Hahahahahahahahahahuhuhahahahahahahaha!* The virtual laughter filled the screen.

I gritted my teeth. Then I flipped the power switch to turn the computer off. It stayed on.

I stamped my foot. These guys were exasperating. Again I had the urge to smash the computer, but I forced myself to control my temper. After all, there were more questions I needed answers to. *What's Brandon Voss doing here? Is he playing the game, too?* I typed.

The answer made me sit up straighter. *No. We're playing the game with you. We just sent some friends of yours along to up the stakes. If you don't get back to the present, they don't, either.*

A surge of anger pulsed through me, followed by a flash of excitement. *Who else is here? How can I find them? Are they old, too?*

*You ask too many questions, Andy,* came the reply. *Think about the clues.* Then the screen went blank.

I sighed and flipped the laptop closed. Things were worse than I'd thought. Not only was I responsible for getting myself back, but I had other people to worry about, too.

I considered e-mailing Amy but decided against it. That

would really knock me out. Much as I wanted to talk to her, I thought I'd wait.

I pulled my jacket tightly around me and sat down cross-legged on the ground. I opened the burlap sack of vegetables I'd taken from Mrs. Van Winkle's house, grabbed a potato, and took a bite. As I chewed, I recited Steve's rhyme to myself.

*Before one hundred you must see*
*The specter by the hanging tree,*
*And meet the woman, cold and pale;*
*Foil them both and do not fail . . .*

I felt a tingle up my spine. The "specter by the hanging tree" must have been John, the ghost. And the "woman, cold and pale" was the ice woman! My heart beat faster. I had done what the rhyme demanded—foiled them both.

I raked a hand through what was left of my hair. At least I had taken some steps in the right direction. Now I had to figure out what to do next. I closed my eyes and recited the rest of the rhyme.

*Then face one final enemy*
*Before you mark a century.*
*Defeat this foe and win the game,*
*Or else it's here you will remain.*

I opened my eyes and rested my chin in my hands. Who was the "final enemy"? I scratched my wrinkled head as I thought.

Then I remembered that Amy had told me to read "The Legend of Sleepy Hollow." I honestly didn't think that some old story we had been assigned in school could really help me figure anything out, but I was totally stumped. So I fished the book out of my pocket and started turning the pages.

Soon I realized Amy had been right. The book *was* some kind of clue. If I had done the homework Mrs. Rathbone had assigned, I would have known enough to detour around the tree where Major André had nearly strangled me.

If I had paid attention, I would have known about the Woman in White—the ice woman. In the story she was the ghost of someone who had died in a snowstorm, and she shrieked on winter nights. Well, that was certainly true.

The creatures in Steve's rhyme were all in "The Legend of Sleepy Hollow," I realized. The Woman in White haunted the glen at Raven Rock. I looked up at the big boulder above me. There were several dark birds sitting on it. They looked like crows to me, but they could have been ravens, I guess. I'm not much into birds.

Now I was really getting hooked on the story. Not only for the information I needed—I actually *liked* it.

I read about Ichabod Crane, who must have been the schoolmaster who had threatened to thrash Brandon Voss. He had a crush on someone named Katrina Van Tassel. *Hmmm,* I thought. *That name sounds familiar.* But why? I couldn't recall knowing anyone by that name at my school . . .

My school. What was the name of my school? I blanked on it. I just couldn't think of the name.

I chewed my lower lip. *Keep reading, keep reading,* I told myself. After all, the thing to remember was that this world I was stuck in wasn't real, and I had to find out how to get back to the present. Once I did that, I hoped my memory would come back.

I forced myself to concentrate on the story of the most frightmarish spirit in Sleepy Hollow: the Headless Horseman.

Whenever anyone had mentioned the Headless Horseman before, I'd always become bored and tried to change the subject. Now that I was living in his neighborhood, however, I wanted to know all I could about him.

Les—my own nickname for *Headless*—was a soldier in the Revolutionary War, just like my friend Major André. But what had happened to Les was even worse than what had happened to the major. Les's head had been shot off by a cannon. When I read that, I had to put the book down for a moment. Anyway, Les's body was buried in a church cemetery.

A chill shot up my spine as I thought of the little church where I had read my own name on a headstone. I somehow knew that it was Les's final resting place, too.

I picked the book up and continued reading. I soon came to a part that made my five or six remaining gray hairs stand straight up on my head. According to the story, Les left the graveyard every night and went prowling around the countryside on his ghost horse in search of his head.

*Great,* I thought. *He could be anywhere at anytime.* The good news was that he only came out at night. By daybreak Les had to be back at the graveyard.

My imagination conjured up all sorts of possibilities for what Les might be up to between the time he left his grave at night and the time he returned to sleep in his coffin, like a vampire.

I came up with lots of gruesome ideas, but the one that made the most sense to me was this: If Les couldn't find his own head, and he still needed one, he'd probably be willing to settle for someone else's. The longer he went without one, the less selective he would become. By now, he'd probably be happy with anyone's head—even mine.

# Chapter 15

I tried to finish reading the story, but my eyes were tired. I kept reminding myself that I was ninety now, and I had to slow down. Then again, if I took it easy, I might be stuck here forever.

The blood started racing through my veins. Someone who looked familiar was walking down the path, not far away. Since I couldn't see very well, I wasn't certain of who it was, but I had a pretty good hunch. Even though I couldn't think of her name, I was pretty sure I knew her in real time.

I stuffed my laptop into my sack—which by now was practically empty of vegetables—stood up, and started toward her. The closer I got, the more convinced I was that I knew this girl. Waving my arms over my head, I shouted, "Hey! Hey, you! Wait up! Stop!"

I was close enough now to see that the girl was very pretty, with long blonde hair. She was wearing a dress with a lot of lace, and plenty of gold jewelry—earrings, rings, necklaces. She turned to look at me, curiosity in her big blue eyes.

"What do you want, old fellow?"

Was I ever sick of being called that! I promised

myself that from now on, whenever I saw an old man, I'd never call him *old fellow, old-timer,* or—the worst—*old geezer.*

"My name is Andy. Andy Winkler. We were in the same class at school."

I knew right away that I'd made an impression. The girl's face went through all sorts of changes—surprise, disbelief, suspicion, and puzzlement.

She tilted her head to one side. "I *did* know someone named Andy Winkler back at Sleepy Hollow. He was kind of cute."

My knees nearly buckled. I never imagined in my wildest dreams that any girl thought of me as "kind of cute"—especially not this one.

"The Andy Winkler I knew was . . . younger. You're too old to be him."

I scuffed my shoe in the dirt. "Yeah, well, things are different here. I know I look older—but I'm still the same Andy Winkler you know. My sister's name is Amy."

That got me a smile. It also got me a tough question. "What's *my* name?"

*Uh-oh.* I groaned inside. My mouth opened. Nothing came out.

"Bye, then."

"Wait!" I blurted. My mind was working furiously. This girl remembered me from real time. I *couldn't* let her get away. *Help me, Amy,* I begged silently.

I don't know if Amy had anything to do with it, but all at once the name popped into my head. I snapped my fingers. "Of course I know your name! You're Katrina Tasselhoff."

Katrina turned and gave me a bigger smile than

before. "You remembered! You *are* Andy Winkler!" She clapped her delicate white hands. Then she turned serious. "You'll have to call me Katrina Van Tassel. That's my name now."

"Okay." I nodded. I would have called her Fred if she had wanted, or anything else, I was so happy to see her. We started walking.

I looked Katrina up and down. "Wow. You look different. I mean, you always looked great—but now you look fantastic!"

Katrina smiled as if she already knew. She nodded at me excitedly. "Yes," she cried. "I'm eighteen here! It's so wonderful!"

"More wonderful than being ninety," I replied. "It looks like you got a lot better deal than I did. Say—how did you get here?"

Katrina shrugged. "I'm not sure. I went home after the Halloween party and went straight to bed. I dreamed I was taking a walk with Brandon. We met those little guys that Rip Van Winkle met before he fell asleep. We all sat around drinking root beer and telling jokes. I remember Brandon and I had a lot of fun in the dream.

"Anyway," she went on, "when I woke up, I was lying in an old-fashioned feather bed. Everybody still called me Katrina, but they said my last name was Van Tassel. Isn't that weird?"

"You don't know the half of it," I said as I rolled my eyes.

"I hated it here at first," she continued. Then she brightened up. "But now I don't. My father is rich! You ought to see our farm. Acres and acres, with all kinds of animals. I have two horses of my own! We have servants, too, and a huge house. My room is twice as big as my bedroom at home. Oh—we even have our own pond. With geese!"

I stared at her. "Your family owns that huge farm I passed by yesterday? I can't believe it! That place is incredible."

"That's right!" Katrina gushed. "It's practically mine! I love it here!"

I shook my head. "Come on, Katrina. You can't mean that. There's nothing to do—no pizza and no video games, no radio, no television. Listen to me. I'm leaving out the most important thing! You must miss your family."

Katrina looked hurt. "Why, of course I miss my family, Andy. It's just . . . I don't know. I have everything I want here—even lots of boyfriends. I'm all grown up. If I went back, I'd be twelve again." She gave her head a little shake. "Twelve isn't this much fun. Besides, I don't know how to get back anyway."

All of a sudden Katrina didn't seem as terrific to me as she once had. She sounded shallow. So what if she was rich and had lots of boyfriends in this place? This wasn't her life. It was the life of some fictitious character! I didn't understand how she could be happier here. I was miserable!

Then Katrina frowned. "The only bad thing is that skinny, funny-looking schoolmaster. He keeps coming over and trying to teach me these stupid old songs. Mr. Van Tassel—I mean, my father—makes me try to sing them because he says a young lady ought to know how to sing. That Ichabod Crane is so goofy!"

"Ichabod Crane!" I exclaimed.

"Ichabod Crane," Katrina echoed. "He hangs around our house all the time." Katrina's full skirt swished as she walked. "There is one guy I like a lot. His name is Brom Bones." She giggled. "At first I thought it was a funny name, but I don't anymore. He has such broad shoulders and dark eyes. I think he's so handsome. I want him to be my boyfriend."

"Would you get real? He's a character in a book!" I wailed. This was getting more and more bizarre. Then my stomach growled and I realized how starved I was. "Say, you must have a lot of food at your house, right?"

Katrina nodded solemnly. "Especially now. We're having a big party tonight. We've got ham and roast beef, peaches and pears, apple pie and pumpkin pie and peach pie, and—"

"Stop!" I said. Hearing about all that food was making me feel faint. "Please, invite an old friend home for a meal."

"Sure. I'll tell Daddy I felt sorry for you."

"Thanks a bunch," I said grimly.

Katrina faced me and put both hands on her hips. "Well, I can't exactly tell him the truth." She turned her mega-blue eyes on me.

I let my breath out with a *whoosh*. "You're right. Tell him whatever you want."

A smile spread across Katrina's features once more. "Good. Then let's go to my place."

She took my arm. We walked past the wheat fields and cornfields on the way to what Katrina now called "my place."

I was pretty psyched about having the chance to set

foot in a house after spending a few days outside—I didn't think I'd ever want to go camping again. By now, I knew I must look—and smell—pretty gross.

All the same, I still felt creeped out. Katrina was acting like she really was Katrina Van Tassel. I wondered how much she remembered about the present. What creeped me out even more was that I knew I was changing, too. More and more, I could feel my memory slipping away. I was starting to actually *feel* ninety instead of twelve.

What was worst of all was that I knew I was forgetting—but it was bothering me less and less. Now that I'd finally spoken to Katrina and I knew she liked me, something inside me had changed. I wasn't as keen to get back to the present, where Katrina didn't seem interested in me.

"We're here!" Katrina announced.

I had been so busy daydreaming that I hadn't noticed we had arrived at the farmhouse.

Katrina gave my sleeve a tug. "We have to go around the back way. I see that geek Ichabod Crane moping around on the porch, waiting for me. Come on." She pulled me along behind her.

Once inside, Katrina led me into a huge kitchen with a fireplace so big that it looked like a cave. The food for the party was laid out on a long table. She let me gorge myself on sandwiches and rich desserts.

"You'll find it's not so bad here," she said while I was eating. At that moment it was hard to disagree. The food in virtual reality was just as good as real food.

Katrina pulled up a chair and sat down next to me. She helped herself to a big slice of peach pie. "You've got to try this," she said, putting another huge slice on my plate. "It's my favorite."

I had to admit that the peach pie was pretty special. While I was stuffing myself, a man around my father's age came into the kitchen.

"Hello, Katrina," he said. "Who is your friend?"

Katrina jumped up. "Hello, Father," she chirped. I swallowed a bite of peach pie and hurriedly wiped my mouth with a napkin.

Katrina turned to me. "Father, this is . . . this is . . ." Katrina's voice trailed off. She looked at me with a vague, unfocused expression. Confusion blurred her delicate features.

My heart sank. *Oh, no,* I thought. *Katrina's forgotten who I am.*

Then a wide smile spread across her face. "Father," she said, "I'd like you to meet my friend, Mr. Rip Van Winkle."

# Chapter 16

"**G**lad to meet you, Mr. Van Winkle," Katrina's "dad" said heartily. He shook my withered old hand. "Please call me Balthus."

"Balthus," I mumbled. I glanced uneasily at Katrina. She was beaming.

"I met Mr. Van Winkle on my way back from the village," she explained. "The poor old fellow was tired and hungry, so I invited him home for some good food and a rest."

I stared at her, stunned. *She really thinks I'm Rip Van Winkle,* I realized.

"You're certainly welcome here, Mr. Van Winkle," Balthus Van Tassel assured me. He patted my shoulder, then plopped a couple of slices of ham on my plate. "Eat up," he said. "Then you can have a nap. Later, I'll send someone to wake you, and if you're up to it, you can come down to the party we're having." He gave me a wink.

*This is all totally weird,* I thought. But I was so hungry, I just kept eating. After I'd eaten my way through a couple more plates of food, Mr. Van Tassel led me upstairs to a room with a fireplace and a huge feather bed.

"You can rest here," he told me.

I looked around at the warm, cozy room. After days of sleeping on the cold ground, it seemed like paradise. I was so thankful I nearly cried.

"See you later, old-timer," Mr. Van Tassel said as he turned to leave. "Sleep well."

When he was gone, I took the laptop out of the burlap sack and put it on the dresser. I thought I should e-mail Amy, but the sight of the feather bed was so tempting that I flung myself down on it. It was like lying on a cloud. I was completely happy.

*Katrina is right,* I thought. *The virtual world isn't so bad.* I closed my eyes. I had planned to lie there for five minutes, then get up and e-mail Amy. Instead, I drifted into a dreamless sleep.

"Mr. Van Winkle! Mr. Van Winkle! Wake up! It's time to get ready for the party!"

The voice seemed to be coming from far away. Someone was shaking me awake.

"No, no! Don't!" I curled up into a ball. "I want to sleep."

"Nonsense!" the voice insisted. "You can't sleep forever. It's time to get ready for the party." I opened one eye and saw a big-boned woman I had never seen before. I would find out later that her name was Helga and that she helped with general cooking and cleaning at the Van Tassel farm.

At first I didn't know where I was. I didn't know who I was, either. This woman was calling me Mr. Van Winkle, so I figured that must be my name.

Helga gave me a glass of milk. Then she showed me

where I could take a bath and where some fresh clothes were laid out for me. I fully enjoyed that bath and the new clothes.

When I had finished dressing, I stood in front of the mirror and told myself I looked pretty good for a man who was nearly one hundred.

That's when it hit me. My brain had flaked out. I had forgotten who I was—for a while.

I stared at the old face in the mirror. "You're not ninety. You're twelve. Your name isn't Rip Van Winkle. It's Andy Winkler. *Don't forget.*"

Just above my shoulder, I caught sight of Helga's face reflected in the mirror. She had gone pale, and her eyes were wide with surprise. Suddenly, her look softened and she burst out laughing.

"You silly old man, talking to yourself in the mirror," she chided. "Just stop that now, and come downstairs to the party."

I thought it best not to argue. Luckily, Helga didn't ask any questions about the laptop on the dresser. Apparently she hadn't noticed it. I didn't argue later, either, when Katrina introduced me to her guests as Mr. Rip Van Winkle. I just wanted to relax, sit in the chair in the corner, and watch the others dance.

There was a guy across the room playing up a storm on a battered fiddle. I found myself tapping my feet in time with the beat. Meanwhile, Ichabod Crane was really kicking up his heels as he danced. He sure had some funny-looking moves.

Even though Katrina had said that she didn't like Ichabod Crane, she didn't seem to mind dancing with him. Every time a dance ended, they danced another one. She batted her eyes at Ichabod, tossed her hair, and giggled at things he said, too.

*No doubt about it,* I thought. *Katrina is flirting like mad with Ichabod Crane.*

It didn't take long to figure out why. There was a man sitting beside me. He was staring at Katrina and Ichabod and sulking. I figured this must be Brom Bones. It seemed as though Katrina was trying to make him jealous. From the looks of things, she was succeeding.

I figured I could learn why Katrina was acting this way if I finished reading "The Legend of Sleepy Hollow." Maybe I could sneak upstairs and peek at the story later to find out how the evening would end.

But after a few moments, I forgot about the book. I was having too good a time. I even got up and clapped my hands and stamped my feet to the music.

The dancing went on until early morning. A bunch of guys, including me, plopped down on the porch, and people started telling scary stories.

It was just the kind of thing I hated in the real world—but now it didn't bother me. When a guy named Brouwer began to tell us about the night he'd seen the Headless Horseman, I hung on his every word.

"Yeah, I saw him all right," Brouwer said quietly. "Huge, he was. He wore a big black cape that ended right here"—he grabbed his neck—"with nothing above it. His horse was as black as his cape, and it had red eyes that burned right through me."

Only Brom Bones looked unimpressed. "So how did you get away from him?"

Brouwer glared. "I don't know. He chased me through

the swamps and over the hills. Then all of a sudden, *bang!* He and his horse both turned into skeletons and jumped up over the treetops."

"Ha!" Brom Bones snorted. "I don't believe you. I think you made that story up." He looked around at every face in the group. "Let me tell you a real story about the Headless Horseman. I met him in the woods last Halloween, near midnight. I challenged him to a race!"

Everyone gasped, including me. Brom Bones grinned broadly.

"The first one to cross the bridge by the old church was to be the winner. My Daredevil was putting that goblin horse to shame, too. But then the Headless Horseman cheated."

There was another gasp from the group. Several of the men looked over their shoulders, as if they were afraid the Headless Horseman might hear his name and get angry.

Brom Bones waited until he had everyone's attention before he went on. "Just as Daredevil and I were about to beat him over the bridge, there was a noise like a thunderclap, and the Headless Horseman vanished in a flash of fire—horse and all."

Everyone was staring at Brom Bones, wide-eyed. Everyone, that is, except Ichabod Crane.

"Stuff and nonsense," the schoolmaster said smugly. "A fireside tale to scare little children. I don't believe you. No intelligent man would, either."

Brom Bones jumped to his feet, his hands doubled into fists. He sprang at Ichabod Crane. The schoolmaster turned to run into the house.

Luckily, Katrina chose that exact moment to glide on-to the porch. "It's almost time for the last dance of the evening," she said sweetly. "Does anybody want to be my partner?"

Every guy in the group jumped up, but Ichabod Crane was the quickest to grab her arm. "It would be my pleasure, dear Katrina," he cooed. He shot Brom Bones a snooty look over his shoulder as he led Katrina back inside. I couldn't help noticing that she didn't look too happy. Brom Bones had a dark scowl on his face.

Through the open door we heard the fiddler strike up the music. Brom Bones pulled his hat down over his eyes and stalked off the porch. I saw him mount his horse and ride off into the night.

After Brom left, the rest of the guys on the porch started to drift away. I hobbled inside and watched Katrina and Ichabod finish the last dance.

"Good night!" Katrina said to Ichabod as soon as the last note died. Ichabod ignored the hint. He stayed close by Katrina's side until all the other guests had left. It wasn't until Mr. Van Tassel told Ichabod "good night" that he slowly turned and left.

"I thought I'd never get rid of him!" Katrina exclaimed a short while later as we got ready to head upstairs to bed. "If I never see him again, it will be too soon," she groaned. "He's such a pest!"

Just then, there was a knock at the door. Katrina's hands flew to the sides of her face. "Oh, no!" she cried. "He's back!"

She ran to Mr. Van Tassel. "You answer the door, please, Father. Tell Ichabod Crane I've gone to bed and I don't ever want to see him again."

Balthus Van Tassel frowned. "Oh, all right. But he's such a nice man," he grumbled.

Mr. Van Tassel opened the front door a crack and peered out. "Why, Brom Bones!" he said in surprise. "You look as if you've seen a ghost! Come in and warm yourself beside the fire."

Brom Bones came in, looking pale and frightened. Katrina flew down the stairs and cheered up at the sight of him. We all sat down to hear his story, which he seemed quite eager to tell.

He pulled his chair up to the fire and began to speak in a hushed voice. "I wasn't far behind Ichabod Crane when he headed for home." He glanced at Katrina. "You know the way we both go, through Wiley's Swamp. It's so dark and gloomy there." He cleared his throat.

"It was at the edge of the swamp that I noticed Ichabod was having trouble with his horse. The poor old nag just didn't want to go any farther, though Ichabod kept kicking her in the ribs."

Brom Bones leaned his elbows on his knees and stared at the floor. "I tried to catch up to him to offer him a ride behind me on Daredevil, but I was too late. I had nearly reached him when I saw it."

"What?" we all whispered.

Brom Bones's head snapped up. "The Headless Horseman!" he thundered. "He took off after Ichabod. The phantom horse was screaming. It was a sound that could wake the dead."

"Oh, no!" Katrina gasped.

"Oh, yes," Brom Bones replied. "Ichabod didn't have a chance. The next thing I saw was the Headless Horseman wrapping Ichabod in his cloak. Then" —Brom squeezed his eyes shut as if what he was about to describe was too terrible to remember—"Ichabod's horse galloped away without him. The Headless Horseman took off in the opposite direction."

"What happened to Ichabod Crane?" Mr. Van Tassel asked.

Brom Bones stared into the fire. "I saw the Headless Horseman gallop away—with Ichabod Crane's head on the pommel of his saddle."

# Chapter 17

The next morning, the first thing I thought about when I opened my eyes was the strange story that Brom Bones had told us the night before. *Poor Ichabod Crane,* I thought. *Now maybe he'll be haunting the place instead of the Headless Horseman, running around at night in search of a new head.*

Somehow, it didn't worry me too much. The schoolmaster just didn't seem the scary type. I figured him for sarcastic, but not fierce.

My gaze rested on a strange something over on the dresser. I was sure I'd never seen anything like it. It didn't seem to be made of wood, brick, clay, or any material I recognized.

I threw back the covers of the feather bed, padded over, and touched it cautiously. It was smooth and cool. Part of it looked like a square piece of glass. Another part had rows of little knobs with letters and numbers and words. Some seemed to contain some strange code or secret language. I read aloud, "Num Lock. Shift." What did it mean? And what were the other knobs—F1, F2, and on up to F12?

I scratched my head. What kind of newfangled

contraption could this be? I peered at it. In one corner were the words *Computek Laptop*. What in tarnation was a Computek Laptop? Maybe it was something Katrina held on her lap to help her sew, I reasoned. But then what was it doing in my room?

I'd have to ask Katrina or Mr. Van Tassel later. Probably when they told me I would find that I'd forgotten something perfectly ordinary, and I'd be embarrassed. Men as old as I was were often foolish and forgetful. I folded the piece of glass down. The thing fit together nicely, like a book.

I washed my face at the washstand, slicked my few strands of hair in place, and dressed. As I put my shirt on, I pressed a hand to my back. Whew! My old bones ached.

Just as I was about to leave my room, I decided to take the Computek Laptop with me. I folded it under my arm and hobbled downstairs.

"Did you sleep well, Mr. Van Winkle?" Helga asked as I took a seat at the table.

"Yup!"

She piled my plate with ham and biscuits. "Do you know what this thing is?" I asked, showing her the odd box.

Helga's round face grew puzzled. "No, can't say as I do," she answered, wrinkling her nose. She reached for it. "I could use it for a doorstop in the kitchen, though."

I pulled the thing away. "First I want to ask Katrina and Mr. Van Tassel if they know anything about it."

Helga put one hand on her hip. "Have it your own way, then," she said as she swished away.

When Katrina and Mr. Van Tassel came down to breakfast, I held up the Computek Laptop. Both of them stared and shook their heads. Neither of them knew what it was, either. "Where on earth did it come from?" Mr. Van Tassel muttered.

"Maybe one of the guests left it," Katrina suggested. She looked especially pretty today, with her blonde hair piled in ringlets on her head. She looked awfully happy about something, too. I wondered what it could be, after last night's tragedy.

Katrina cast a sidelong look at her father and blushed. "After you went upstairs, Mr. Van Winkle, Brom told us the truth. The Headless Horseman didn't take Ichabod's head at all. He wasn't even near Ichabod last night!

"It was Brom, dressed up like the Headless Horseman," she continued. "Brom chased Ichabod and scared him to death. He told him never to come back to Sleepy Hollow. He wanted him to stay away from me!" Katrina was glowing.

I swallowed a biscuit. "Then how come he told us that the Headless Horseman rode off with Ichabod Crane's head?"

Katrina looked at me as if she thought I was the biggest dunce in the world. "Because he wanted to see how much I cared for Ichabod. He had to find out before he asked me to marry him."

I nearly choked. "*Marry?* You're too young to get married, Katrina. You've got to finish school."

Now Mr. Van Tassel looked at me like I was crazy. "School? Katrina doesn't go to school. Eighteen is plenty old enough to get married, and Brom Bones is a good catch for a girl."

I decided I'd better not say anything else. I kept quiet and finished eating.

After breakfast I took the Computek Laptop upstairs. As I put it back on the dresser, I couldn't stop staring at it. As I ran my hand along its side, my thumb tripped some kind of a lever.

*Boom!* The thing lit up all of a sudden. Light flashed in the piece of glass and then the machine started to hum.

"It's alive!" I gasped as I jumped away.

Words flashed on the square of glass. *Mail is waiting*.

I didn't want to get near the thing, but it seemed to pull me closer. I could tell it wanted me to do something, but what?

I poked at a couple of little buttons. *Beep! Beep!* The thing made noises.

I jumped again as letters appeared on the glass.

*Andy, where are you? Why don't you answer? I found out what you have to do to get back.*

Now I wasn't so much scared as mystified. Who was Andy? Where was he, and where did he have to get back to?

I had a terrifying thought. Was this Andy trapped inside the Computek Laptop?

I picked up the contraption and peered at it. I shook it a little bit. No little person fell out.

I couldn't stop staring at the screen. Something was happening to me. The room started to blur. I reached out and grabbed the edge of the dresser. *Hold on, old man,* I told myself.

The name *Amy* began to repeat itself in my mind, as if someone were whispering to me. *Amy, Amy, Amy, Amy*.

Everything got all jumbled up in my brain. I saw myself as a baby, a teenager, an old man. Memories exploded in my head like quick flashes of light.

I opened my eyes. *Wow*. I had nearly forgotten who I was. *I'm Andy*. Somehow the laptop had found me again. Somehow Amy had reached out to me and helped me get the memories back.

I felt lightheaded, and my knees were weak. There wasn't a moment to spare. I began typing a message to Amy.

*Amy, I'm here. I'll explain what happened later. What have you found out?*

A message appeared almost immediately. *You're not going to like it.*

*Never mind. I don't like anything that's happened.*

*The only way out is—*

The last part of the message was wiped out. After a moment new words filled the screen.

*Andy, you've been cheating! You weren't supposed to communicate with the outside world. Sorry, we've crashed your hard drive. Your e-mail function has been wiped out. The magic number is now ninety-nine. You'll be one hundred years old tomorrow. And unless you act quickly, you'll have to stay here forever.*

# Chapter 18

I spied Katrina passing by in the hallway outside my room. *"Psst! Psst!"* I called. "Hey, get in here." I dashed out and grabbed her by the wrist.

She looked like she definitely wanted to be somewhere else. "Are you all right, Mr. Van Winkle? You don't look at all well."

"Look, my name isn't—forget it. Just come in and let me talk to you for a minute. It's important. There are some things you're totally clueless about, and I've got to bring you up to speed."

Katrina's eyes widened. "What language are you speaking?" She shot me a look, but she followed me into my room.

As soon as I had closed the door, I started to explain. "Listen, Katrina. You can't marry this Brom Bones character. I'm sure he's a nice guy and all, but he's not real, and you are."

"What?" Katrina's jaw dropped.

"Let me finish. You're from another world. Another reality, I mean. You were brought here, to cyberspace, by some strange little men. You've lost your memory, but you've got to believe me. You and I are both twelve years old, and we go to the same school." I felt a pang of guilt. "It's all my fault. They brought you here because of me."

I stopped babbling to catch my breath. Katrina was staring at me, wide-eyed. I couldn't blame her. What would I have thought a few days ago if someone told me the same story?

Then she glanced at the computer. She ran over to it and read the words that were still on the screen. *"Crashed . . . hard drive . . . e-mail function."* Her eyes narrowed. Then she gasped. "I know what's happened, Mr. Van Winkle! This is some kind of magic. It has put a spell on you!" she cried.

Before I could stop her, she grabbed the computer with both hands, held it high over her head for a few seconds, and flung it to the floor. It smashed to bits.

*Now the computer is* really *crashed,* I thought grimly as I bent down to collect the pieces.

Katrina ran from the room and came back a moment later with Mr. Van Tassel. She rattled on a mile a minute as she told him what I'd just said. Then she pointed to the smashed computer.

Mr. Van Tassel looked pretty freaked out, too. He ordered me to get out of the house immediately. To make sure I followed instructions, he chased me out the front door and even threw a couple of shoes at me!

As I left, I was feeling pretty down. I hadn't the faintest idea how to get back to the present. The computer was smashed, so I couldn't communicate with Amy anymore. Besides that, I was completely exhausted again. How was I going to figure out anything if I fell asleep?

I tried to fight the fatigue, but it was no use. I barely managed to drag myself around to the back of the house, where I snuck into some bushes and collapsed on the hard ground.

My last thought before being swept into a fitful sleep was that come tomorrow, I would be one hundred years old—and I'd be stuck here forever.

# Chapter 19

Almost immediately I was plunged into a strange dream that seemed very real—and very creepy, too.

Amy had somehow been transported to this cyber world, but she wouldn't speak to me. We were walking toward a dingy, scary-looking house made of gray stone. The yard was choked with weeds, and the massive oak trees that surrounded the house were all dead. The windows were so caked with dust and dirt that we couldn't see inside.

"What are we doing here?" I whispered to Amy. She held her finger to her lips, motioning for quiet, and then pointed to the mailbox. I wiped a layer of dirt off the side. The letters on the mailbox were so old-fashioned and full of curlicues that I could hardly read the name. After staring at the letters for several minutes I finally figured it out: *Millie Knickerbocker.*

*Who in the world is Millie Knickerbocker?* I was about to ask Amy that question, but she put a hand over my mouth. With her other hand she motioned for me to go on inside. I wanted her to come with me, but she vanished before my eyes.

Somehow I knew that Amy was trying to tell me

something through the dream. Maybe she was trying to tell me the rest of her e-mail message. Still, it was all very spooky.

I pulled open the huge wooden door and stepped inside. The place was like a cave. Only a few fingers of pale light managed to fight their way through the filthy windows.

The door slammed shut with a terrifying crash so loud that I jumped. I felt like a prisoner. Then a soft voice reached out to me through the darkness.

"May I help you? I believe there is something you need to know."

In a moment my eyes adjusted to the dimness. I looked around and gasped. There were bats hanging from the rafters, staring at me with their bloodthirsty, beady little eyes. The glass eyes of a stuffed owl were staring at me, too.

"Don't be afraid." The soft voice spoke again. "They're friends."

Then I saw a small, strange-looking woman sitting on a worn sofa. Her face was perfectly round, and so were her eyes, which darted this way and that like a lizard's. Her hair was frizzy and a brilliant shade of red.

"I'm Millie Knickerbocker," she said as she got up and came over to welcome me. "My ancestor, Diedrich Knickerbocker, knew a great many mysterious things about the early days of Sleepy Hollow." She looked at me with those lizardlike eyes of hers. They never stopped moving.

I remembered that when Washington Irving wrote about Sleepy Hollow, he always put a note at the end of each story about how he got the information from

Diedrich Knickerbocker. But Mrs. Rathbone told us it was only part of the story. There wasn't really a Diedrich Knickerbocker.

"Uh, I thought Diedrich Knickerbocker was just someone Washington Irving made up, like Rip Van Winkle and Ichabod Crane," I said.

The words slithered from Millie Knickerbocker's throat. "Well, then, you're a very confused young man. Those people were all real—once."

"I'm Andy Winkler," I said when I was able to speak again. "Something really weird and awful has happened to me. I know it sounds nuts, but I've been kidnapped by three little guys who look like trolls —and I'm trapped in the past. Well, not exactly the past. More like virtual reality. I'm trapped in 'The Legend of Sleepy Hollow,' except that some things are different than they were in the story, and—"

"Stop!" snapped Millie. "I know all about your problem, so don't waste time trying to explain."

I felt like somebody had just thrown a bucket of icy water over me. I had to stop talking because I was speechless anyway.

Millie sighed. "I was afraid that something like this would happen. Those awful little fellows do something terrible every Halloween."

I watched as the strange woman got up, walked to the front door, and locked it. Then she motioned for me to follow her.

She took me into a tiny, windowless room in the back of the house. Dusty wooden bookshelves lined the walls, and there were books piled everywhere—ancient-looking books thickly coated with dust. Millie took a seat behind an old, battered desk. I sat in a chair on the other side. I didn't dare say a word, so I waited for her to speak.

Meanwhile, I let my eyes wander. I couldn't help noticing there was a human skull on the corner of the desk. A snake was crawling over and over it, around and around, in and out of the eyes. I told myself I *must not* get sick.

The snake stopped, seeming to notice me for the first time. It looked at me, lashed its forked tongue out, and emitted a threatening *hiss*. I jumped in my chair.

Millie cackled. "That's Alfred. He only hisses when he sees someone, or something, unfamiliar. He'll be used to you in a few minutes."

I settled back into my chair and watched Alfred warily as Millie talked. "Those little fellows who kidnapped you have been around for centuries. They put a horrible spell on Sleepy Hollow all those years ago," she said.

I nodded and held my breath as a rat—*a rat!*—skittered across the desk. Millie Knickerbocker didn't bat a reptilian eye. For the first time, I noticed that the bookshelves were swarming with mice. I squirmed in my chair.

"My ancestor, Diedrich, found out their secrets," she went on.

"How did he do that?" I burst out.

Millie's thin, clawlike hand darted out and grabbed my wrist. "Don't ask!" she whispered. "Some things are better left unsaid, because it's dangerous to know them. Look what happened to Diedrich."

*What?* I wondered. Silence hung in the air.

"He disappeared one Halloween," she said finally, when I didn't think I could stand the suspense one second more. "He went out to buy a cake and was never seen again."

For some reason this struck me funny, and I had to work really hard not to crack a smile. I knew that if I did Millie would make something terribly, unspeakably awful happen to me. Maybe even worse than what had happened already.

Then she actually smiled at me, kind of pulling back the corners of her lipless mouth toward her ears. It made her look a whole lot creepier than when she didn't smile, and I was really glad when she stopped. I was also glad that she let go of my wrist.

"These little creatures love nothing more than playing games." She looked at me meaningfully. "It's what they live for. In fact, without the games, they can't exist." She paused for a moment and then added, "They cheat, of course."

"Oh, I know that!" The words leaped out of my mouth. I drew back, expecting Millie to go for me with a claw, but she didn't. She didn't even seem to mind my speaking up this time.

"It's the cheating you have to watch out for," she continued. "That business of changing the rules, turning things around. But it can't be helped." Her eyes swiveled in their sockets.

Millie tapped the leather cover of a heavy book with a broken fingernail. "This is the journal of Diedrich Knickerbocker. In it is all the information you need to break the spell that the little pranksters put on Sleepy Hollow all those years ago." She smiled again, and I had to look away.

*How could the journal contain everything I need to*

*know to break the spell if the little guys keep cheating and breaking the rules?* I wondered.

"You're wondering how you can break the spell if the trolls keep changing the rules," Millie said. I snapped up straighter in my chair. "There's no guarantee you'll succeed." She shrugged. "You're also wondering why the trolls picked you."

I *had* been wondering that in the back of my mind. "I didn't even believe in them," I said.

Millie looked thoughtful for a moment. "Maybe that's why you were chosen. They wanted to teach you a lesson. I'll tell you something else. They always pick someone they think is a worthy opponent. Remember, to them the game is everything."

A rat crawled across the desk again. Millie swatted it with her palm and sent it flying through the air. It bounced off the bookshelf and raced into a corner. She wiped her hand against her skirt.

*Ugh,* I thought.

Millie's clawlike fingers slowly opened Diedrich Knickerbocker's journal. The ancient binding groaned as she turned to a page near the end of the book. "Now, let's get down to business. I'll tell you what you have to do to win. But be warned that there is less than one chance in a million you'll be able to do it."

*Thanks for the vote of confidence,* I thought.

"Don't be snotty," Ms. Knickerbocker hissed. "Pay attention."

"I'm all ears."

She looked at me sharply, then began to read. After several minutes she said, "You have to destroy the Headless Horseman."

I jumped from my chair. "You're crazy!" I shouted.

"Sit down this instant!" Millie barked. Her voice pushed me back into the chair.

"If you destroy the Headless Horseman, the spell over Sleepy Hollow will be broken. The little trolls will be destroyed, along with all the creatures they created to haunt this place. That's the way they set up the game. They play for keeps—and you'll have to, as well." Millie Knickerbocker leaned toward me, her weird eyes boring into mine. I couldn't turn away.

"If you fail, not only will the spell remain, but you will become theirs, to do with as they choose. And it won't be pleasant." She sniffed. "Now, are you ready to listen?"

I nodded. "Y-yes."

"All right, then. Forget those stories you heard from that Brouwer fellow and Brom Bones. Nobody has ever escaped the Headless Horseman. He's got hundreds of heads. You know, he isn't out hunting for his own head when he leaves the graveyard at night. He's hunting for new ones to add to his collection."

She paused to let this information sink in. "Every night the Headless Horseman crosses the bridge near the church to begin his search. He must return to the graveyard by daybreak, or he will be destroyed. You have to prevent him from recrossing the bridge before the sun starts to come up. If he is still on the bridge when the sun begins to rise, your troubles are over. You can get back to the present through the same passageway that brought you here."

My head snapped up. "Huh? I thought if the spell was broken, I'd just wake up in the present. How can my troubles be over if I'm stuck floating around in cyberspace?"

Millie closed the heavy journal. "You're being very tiresome. I said that you could go back the same way you came in."

I jumped from my chair again. "That's just it. I came in through a computer somehow. Now I don't have one—it was smashed."

My mouth dropped open with a sudden horrifying thought. "And what about the others from the present? My friends Katrina and Brandon are here, too. They don't have computers either. They've even forgotten who they are. How will they get back?" It was stretching it to say Brandon was my friend, but I figured we were in this together.

Millie drummed her fingers on the desk. "The trolls are playing the game with you, so, obviously, the outcome is up to you. If you get back, everyone else does, too."

Millie took my arm and led me toward the front door. I want to give you a gift. You can choose one thing in my house to take with you."

"Wait a minute," I protested. "You didn't tell me how to keep the Headless Horseman from crossing the bridge before sunrise!"

Millie drew back and scowled at me. Her horrible lizard eyes looked like they were about to pop out of her head. "I've already told you everything you need to know to lift the curse." She spit out the words. "Think about everything I've said. I offered you a gift. Now take it and get going."

I took a quick look around the big, old, creepy place.

I couldn't think of a thing I wanted to take away from there—at first. Then I had an idea. I ran back into the office.

"Good choice," Millie said when I returned.

"I'll leave you with this thought," she rasped as she let me out. "For centuries, people have tried to destroy the Headless Horseman. Of all those who have tried, not one has ever been seen again."

# Chapter 20

"They were never seen again, they were never seen again," I heard myself chanting as I struggled to come out of the dream. Then, suddenly, I jerked awake.

I had never experienced a night like this. It was straight out of every spooky Halloween story I'd ever heard. Fog hung everywhere, lit up by the full moon so that it looked like glittering cobwebs. The windows of the farmhouse were dark, and the air was still. The only noises came from the night creatures—the hooting of owls and screeching of bats.

I struggled to my feet. I felt charged with electricity in spite of my ninety-nine years. I wondered how long that energy would last.

A sudden thought made me check my pocket. Good. The gift I'd taken from Millie's office was still there, ready to use when the time came. I'd have to use it then—not a moment sooner. For a second I was glad I was in virtual reality—otherwise, how could my dream gift still be in my pocket when I awoke?

I took a deep breath. *I might as well get started,* I thought. Making my way by the eerie light, I walked toward the church graveyard, the resting place of the

Headless Horseman. Every bush, every rock, and every tree seemed to be watching me, waiting to pounce.

As I headed into the thick woods the Headless Horseman regularly patrolled, the air came alive with the beating of wings. At least a hundred ravens must have flown from Raven Rock. Their cries sounded like human shrieks.

But there was no wailing from the Woman in White. *Did I really destroy her,* I wondered, *or is she just quiet because it isn't snowing?* Strangely enough, I almost didn't want to think of her as gone.

*They'll all be gone when I've finished with the Headless Horseman,* I thought. I crossed my fingers and hoped that was the way things would turn out.

My feet caught on some brambles. For an instant I thought someone had reached out and grabbed me by the ankles. My heart thudded in my chest.

Even by the light of the full moon, these woods were dark and gloomy. I'd have to be very watchful. My eyes searched the darkness. I crept forward softly, listening. The crunch of twigs underneath my feet echoed in my ears.

I came to a part of the woods where the bare tree branches laced together overhead so tightly that even with the light of the full moon, I could hardly see my hands in front of my face. The light was so dim that I had stepped ankle-deep in a brook before I saw it. Then I realized I had been listening so hard for some sign of the Headless Horseman that I hadn't even heard the noise of the water as it ran over the stones.

Now I heard the brook whispering a warning to me. *Be careful, Andy. He's out here, looking for you. He's out here, waiting for you—waiting to tear your head off your neck.*

Although the night was clear and cold, sweat ran down my face. I felt as if I had just finished running a marathon.

In spite of the darkness I was sure I saw a shadow. Its huge form towered over me, and it was darker than the night.

My body started to tremble. *It's him. I know it.*

Somehow I forced myself to keep walking. The dark shape moved right alongside me.

The woods began to thin out a little, but it was still too dark to see more than a few feet ahead. Still, I could sense the shadow following along, waiting for the right moment to strike.

Suddenly a bolt of lightning slashed across the sky. For a split second the darkness was replaced by bright light, and I saw him—not just a big, dark shape, but the whole fearful figure. He was gigantic, mounted on a huge, magnificent black horse with terrifying, burning red eyes.

The horse reared on its hind legs, towering above me, and the rider rose in his stirrups. His dark cloak billowed around him. There was a horrible empty space where his head should have been.

The horse's hooves came down so close that they nearly hit me, and then the animal reared again and neighed—except the neigh was really a horrible groan. The Headless Horseman slashed at the air around me with his sword, and I ducked just in time to avoid being struck.

I scrambled away, and the horseman began chasing me, his black cloak flying out behind him. At least I had an advantage—the tree trunks and stumps were so thick that the horse had to keep dodging right and left and couldn't pick up any speed.

I was glad to find that the ghostly horse and rider couldn't just go right through the trees. Maybe some ghosts can walk through doors and anything else that's solid, but this one couldn't. It was a big relief, let me tell you.

I was able to keep a hair's length away from the Headless Horseman and his terrifying sword. It sliced through the air around my head again and again. The horse's hooves moved silently over the ground, and I felt its hot breath on my neck.

I ran as if my body were only twelve again and I was the fastest runner in the sixth grade. My energy seemed to come from a bottomless pit, but I knew it really came from Amy. She was sending me everything she had.

As we drew nearer to the bridge, I began to pray for another bolt of lightning. The horse had to be able to see clearly or my plan wouldn't work.

Finally my feet struck the wooden surface of the bridge. The Headless Horseman was close behind.

My heart sank as clouds covered the moon. The sword slashed the air, once, twice, then again. The last time, it sliced through the fabric of my jacket.

Not until we were in the middle of the bridge did luck finally smile on me. Several jagged bolts of lightning cut the sky, one after the other.

There wasn't a moment to lose. I turned and faced the beast with the burning eyes, ripping my gift from my pocket. I held it high, right in front of the horse's face so it couldn't help but see.

Alfred the snake didn't fail me. As another bolt of lightning cracked the sky, he drew back his head, his tongue lashing from his mouth, and let out a loud, menacing hiss as his jaws gaped open.

A high, terrible shriek of panic tore from the horse's throat. It reared up on its hind legs and twisted away, bucking again and again. The Horseman's hands sawed at the reins, but it did no good. The terrified animal was out of control.

The horse threw its head around desperately. Finally the rider was thrown off, and the horse streaked away into the night. I tucked Alfred back in my pocket.

Now we were alone, the Headless Horseman and I. The ghostly soldier slashed the air with his sword, but without the eyes of the horse he was lost. He staggered around blindly.

Moments later, the sun dawned on the horizon. Exhausted, I watched as the light fell on the Headless Horseman. Then I gasped.

For the briefest instant a head appeared on his shoulders. He opened his mouth and let out a horrible, bloodcurdling scream. Then the flesh began to melt away. His clothes turned to tatters and fell from his bones. In a matter of seconds all that was left was a skeleton.

As the sky lit up, the skeleton of the Headless Horseman let out another horrible scream. Then I watched as the fiercest, most feared ghost of Sleepy Hollow vanished in a huge explosion of fire.

No sooner did the first flames lick the sky than the ground beneath my feet began to shake faster and faster, until it was breaking apart. It felt as if I were in the middle of an earthquake—but it wasn't an earthquake.

The spell had been broken. The virtual world the trolls had created was destroying itself. And I was caught in the middle of the destruction.

Huge crevices cracked the ground, leaving deep, yawning gashes. Powerful forces whipped around me, tugging at me until I was afraid I was going to break apart. The air roared with noise louder than a hundred rumbling cracks of thunder.

Then suddenly, everything got very still . . . except for me. I felt myself being spun around into a whirling, twisting cloud of light. Colors and shapes sped by in dazzling brilliance. I was swept along, flying through space and time.

As I flew, I knew where the energy was coming from. It was Amy. I could feel her mind touching mine. The energy of our minds had joined together in a force powerful enough to carry me out of cyberspace and back to the present.

# Chapter 21

From the courtyard of Washington Irving Junior High School, I watched the little kids in Halloween costumes terrorizing everyone on the blacktop of Sleepy Hollow Elementary next door. There were still the same ghosts, goblins, and headless horsemen as there had been the year before. I was happy to see that there were some new costumes, too—like robots and space aliens.

Katrina Tasselhoff and Brandon Voss passed by. "Hi, Andy." Katrina batted her eyes.

"Hey, man!" Brandon slapped me on the shoulder. "See you tonight."

Neither one of them remembered our adventure together, but ever since it had happened, our relationship had changed. Brandon thought of me as one of his best buds, and Katrina flirted with me all the time.

I guess it was because of the way I had changed. Defeating the Headless Horseman had given me loads of confidence. Many others had tried and failed—but I had done it! I never got nervous and tongue-tied the way I used to. In fact, these days I thought I was the coolest guy in school.

Unfortunately, Amy didn't agree. She kept telling me

I had become somewhat obnoxious since my return from cyberspace.

"Hey, bro." Amy came and stood next to me. "I'll bet you're thinking about last year."

"You've got it," I said. We both looked off into the distance. I knew neither one of us would ever forget—and we'd never tell another soul. They'd lock us up and throw away the keys!

In a last little twist of space and time, things had somehow worked out so that no one's parents realized their kids had been gone for days. That was because all the days we'd been caught in cyberspace seemed like only hours to everyone on earth—everyone except Amy, that is. Because of the connection between us, she alone knew what had really happened. To everyone else, it was as if Brandon, Katrina, and I had simply gone to sleep and awakened in our own beds the next morning.

Nobody ever mentioned Steve, Mark, and Ray. The teacher never even read their names out at roll call anymore. It was as if they had never existed.

The part that Amy and I couldn't figure out was Millie Knickerbocker. While doing some research at the library, Amy had found out about her in an old book called *Mysterious Sleepy Hollow*. Amy had wanted to e-mail me the stuff she had learned in that book, but Steve had crashed my e-mail function. So Amy tried to send me a dream—it was the only way she could think of to communicate with me. That was when I had dreamed about Millie.

*Mysterious Sleepy Hollow* had said that Millie was the last living relative of Diedrich Knickerbocker, and even listed her address. A few days after I got back, we went to pay Millie a visit. But when we arrived, there was only a Big Scoop's Forty-Nine Flavors ice cream store at that address. Then we went back to search for the old book at the library, but the librarian said there was no book called *Mysterious Sleepy Hollow*!

As long as the spell on Sleepy Hollow had been lifted, it really didn't matter, but I would have liked to thank Millie for her help. She was certainly strange, but I couldn't have done it without her.

So much had changed in the past year. I was a teenager now, and I felt so much older—not to mention cooler. Tonight I wasn't going to a kids' Halloween costume party. I was going to a horror film festival with Katrina and Brandon.

Another thing that had changed was the way I felt about the past. I still liked to talk about the future, but ever since I'd come back from cyberspace, history had been my best subject.

Later that night, after I got home from the film festival, I tiptoed up the stairs. The door to my room was open a crack. A greenish glow spilled out into the hall. I crept forward and slowly pushed back the door.

The greenish glow was coming from my computer monitor. My breath caught in my throat. I hadn't left my computer on. I *knew* it.

Then I noticed a second odd thing. The home page for the Halloween chat room *Holloween* was on my monitor. I stared at the picture of the Headless Horseman.

This was really weird. I happened to know that the home page for *Holloween* wasn't the Headless Horseman this year. It was a spooky graveyard. So what was this picture doing on the screen?

As I stared, the Headless Horseman seemed to come alive. The horse reared up on its hind legs and let out that awful noise I remembered. Its burning red eyes bored into my own.

I began to shake all over. Suddenly the image of the horse on the screen seemed to fill the room. And then . . . the horse came galloping toward me. The Headless Horseman's sword slashed the air.

I screamed in terror. "This can't be happening! I destroyed you! I saw you burst into flames!"

Deafening, evil laughter surrounded me, and the image of the Headless Horseman vanished. The faces of the three trolls appeared on the screen. Steve grinned and shook his head. Then a message marched across the screen.

*Sorry, Andy. We cheated again. Now you'll have to play another game.*

# Don't miss any of these exciting books!

| | | |
|---|---|---|
| _____ | 0-8167-4279-0 | #1 Meltdown Man |
| _____ | 0-8167-4280-4 | #2 Lost in Dino World |
| _____ | 0-8167-4343-6 | #3 Virtual Nightmare |
| _____ | 0-8167-4344-4 | #4 Invasion of the Body Thieves |
| _____ | 0-8167-4427-0 | #5 Double Trouble _(Oct. '97)_ |
| _____ | 0-8167-4428-9 | #6 Visitor from the Beyond _(Oct. '97)_ |

### $3.95 each

_Available at your favorite bookstore . . ._
_or use this form to order by mail._

Please send me the books I have checked above. I am enclosing $_____ (please add $2.00 for shipping and handling). Send check or money order payable to Troll Communications — no cash or C.O.D.s, please — to Troll Communications, Customer Service, 2 Lethbridge Plaza, Mahwah, NJ 07430.

Name _____

Address_____

City _____State_____ZIP _____

Age _____ Where did you buy this book? _____

Please allow approximately four weeks for delivery. Offer good in the U.S. only. Sorry, mail orders are not available to residents of Canada. Price subject to change.

# In your travels...

# VISIT PLANET TROLL

## An out-of-this-world Web site!

**Check out Kids' T-Zone where you can:**

- Get FREE stuff—visit FreeZone for details
- Win prizes
- Send e-mail greeting cards to your friends
- Play trivia games
- Order books on-line

# Enter our galaxy for the ultimate fun experience!

# http://www.troll.com